Twelve ...
Twelve indomitable heroines.
One UNIFORMLY HOT! miniseries.

Don't miss a story in Harlequin Blaze's first
12-book continuity series, featuring irresistible
soldiers from all branches of the armed forces.

First up are those sexy men of the U.S. Army...

THE REBEL
by Rhonda Nelson
January 2011

BREAKING THE RULES
by Tawny Weber
February 2011

IN THE LINE OF FIRE
by Jennifer LaBrecque
March 2011

*And don't miss the hot heroes of the U.S. Navy,
showing up for duty next month!*

Uniformly Hot!
The Few. The Proud. The Sexy as Hell.

Available wherever Harlequin books are sold.

Blaze

Dear Reader,

Every now and then, an author is lucky enough to come up with a story in which everything falls into place. That's what happened to me during this book. I love the Uniformly Hot series, I adore a runaway bride story and I can't help cheering for two people who have been in love with one another forever, but their timing was never right... until now. And *In the Line of Fire* gave me the chance to combine all three....

Major Colton Sawyer has stayed away from his best friend's little sister for reasons of his own personal honor. Andi Mitchell has had a crush on her big brother's best friend ever since she hit her teens. But she thought she was over him. In fact, she was even ready to marry someone else...until Colton showed up at the wedding.

I hope you enjoy Colton and Andi's adventurous path to true love. Please stop by to visit me at www.jenniferalabrecque.com.

Happy reading!

Jennifer LaBrecque

Jennifer LaBrecque

IN THE LINE OF FIRE

TORONTO NEW YORK LONDON
AMSTERDAM PARIS SYDNEY HAMBURG
STOCKHOLM ATHENS TOKYO MILAN MADRID
PRAGUE WARSAW BUDAPEST AUCKLAND

Recycling programs
for this product may
not exist in your area.

ISBN-13: 978-0-373-79602-1

IN THE LINE OF FIRE

Copyright © 2011 by Jennifer LaBrecque

ABOUT THE AUTHOR

After a varied career path that included barbecue-joint waitress, corporate numbers cruncher and bug-business maven, Jennifer LaBrecque has found her true calling writing contemporary romance. Named 2001 Notable New Author of the Year and 2002 winner of the prestigious Maggie Award for Excellence, she is also a two-time RITA® Award finalist. Jennifer lives in suburban Atlanta with a Chihuahua who runs the whole show.

Books by Jennifer LaBrecque

HARLEQUIN BLAZE

1

HE'D DAMN WELL RATHER face a firing squad than escort Andromeda "Andi" Mitchell down the aisle at her wedding and "give her away" to another man. U.S. Army Major Colton Sawyer propped his booted feet on the edge of the makeshift table in his barracks in Afghanistan. "That's not going to work," he said over the dismal phone connection to his buddy Rion Mitchell.

Rion, also stationed in Afghanistan but at a different base, said, "Colton, my leave's been denied. You know how the army can be. There's no rhyme or reason to some of these decisions." There truly was no rationale sometimes behind whether one soldier was denied leave and another granted his or hers. Rion and Colton had both applied for leave to attend Rion's sister's wedding and catch up. "I can't walk her down the aisle if I'm not there so you're the next best thing, bro. You've gotta stand in for me."

Colton rubbed the back of his neck with his right hand. Dammit. He and Rion had grown up next door to one another. Not only were their mothers best friends, he and Rion had been best friends since diaperdom. They were closer than brothers. Growing up, Colton had spent as much time at the Mitchell house as his own, and vice versa.

When Rion's father was killed in a car crash in Florida en route to a conference, fifteen-year-old Colton had grieved as deeply as the Mitchell family over the loss. The entire Sawyer family had been bereft over the loss of their dear friend. Gerald Mitchell, an astronomy professor, had named his children Andromeda and Orion and even given Colton his own honorary constellation name of Pyxis. He'd claimed Colton should be known as the "compass" because a person could always count on Colton's course to be steady. But this was one time he simply couldn't stay the course….

He grasped at another solution. "What about your cousin Eli? It should be a family member."

"Eli lives in some remote town in Alaska," Rion countered. "I'm sure he won't be flying in from Good Riddance or wherever the hell he lives just for Andi's wedding. And you're like family. C'mon, Pyxis," he said. "If Dad could handpick someone to replace him and me in this role, you know he'd say you."

Damn, Rion. He could sell an Eskimo an icemaker

in December. "Yeah, well, how's your mother going to feel about this?"

No one ever called it a nervous breakdown, but in retrospect that's exactly what had happened to Daisy Mitchell following her husband's death. She'd gotten better, but she'd never, ever been the same. She had an almost obsessive compulsion to not let Andi and Rion out of her sight. The family vacations the Mitchells and Sawyers had taken together became a thing of the past. Obviously her fears were driven by Gerald's death while he was traveling—in Daisy's world, the only safe place was Savannah.

Colton had known from the time he was a boy he wanted a military career. He'd known his calling was to serve and protect. He'd never made any secret of it and had joined ROTC the minute he could sign up for it in school. Rion had joined as well but had never seemed particularly interested in making the military his career. However, during his senior year that all shifted and he had decided the army was the route he wanted to take, as well. Sure, as best friends he and Rion had discussed Rion's options and his decision, but Colton hadn't swayed him one way or the other. However, when Rion announced his decision to leave Savannah and join the army after college, Daisy had suffered another minibreakdown. And somewhere along the way she'd figured Colton was to blame for what she saw as her son's desertion. She'd never come right out and said it, but she'd implied it to him more than once and he'd never quite felt welcome in her home again. He couldn't imagine she'd want him walking Andi down the aisle.

"Mom'll be fine with it." Colton could almost see Rion's nonchalant shrug. "I keep thinking Andi will change her mind."

Something inside him suspended at Rion's declaration even though it wouldn't change Colton's situation. "Why would you think that?"

"I just don't think he's the right guy for her. I don't know that he appreciates her fun-loving spirit. Hell, I don't think Andi's really in love with him. I think she's settling for someone she likes well enough but then what the hell do I know, I only met the dude once."

Colton felt twisted inside. He wanted Andi to be happy. "You picked a helluva time to bring it up now when she's getting married in two weeks." And in part that was because Colton went out of his way *not* to discuss Andi with Rion. Rion knew him too well. For years now, Andi had been a topic best avoided, in Colton's opinion.

"Yeah, well, Andi's got to make her own choices. We all have to make our own choices, don't we, and then live with the consequences?" Rion was known to make the cryptic comment now and then. "So, c'mon, Pyxis, as an honorary member of the Mitchell family, say you'll fill in for me and walk Andi down the aisle to give her away to rising junior bank executive Blanton Prichard."

Rion's words were like a knife twisting in his gut but all of Colton's viable arguments were gone and the truth wasn't an option, in his book. Truer words had never been spoken that often the right thing to do wasn't the easy thing. He closed his eyes and resigned himself to the necessary task. "Okay, I'll do it."

"Cool. I knew I could count on you."

Colton had just agreed to walk down the aisle with the woman he loved…so she could marry another man.

"Is HE HERE?" Andi asked when Martha Anne Sawyer, Colton's mother, walked into the grand ballroom of the Whitfield Mansion where the Friday evening wedding rehearsal was wrapping up.

Andi had had butterflies in her stomach throughout the entire thing. She was sure it was because, well, she was going to be married tomorrow and *not* because she was anxious or excited or nervous or any of the above about seeing Colton Sawyer again for the first time in several years. Granted, he'd broken her heart into little pieces but that had been her own private business. He hadn't meant to because a man like Colton would never deliberately break anyone's heart, unlike a whole lot of other guys out there.

No, he'd broken her heart because he'd never seemed to know she existed as anything other than

Rion's pain-in-the-ass little sister. God, she'd had a crush on him since she was a kid. And she thought she'd outgrown it until her freshman year at the Savannah College of Art and Design, when she was nineteen and he was twenty-five and he'd come home on leave.

It had been horrible and wonderful and everything in between. She'd fallen so madly, passionately in love with him, without the slightest indication he saw her as anything other than the girl next door. She'd also been terrified. He was about to ship out as one of the earliest deployments to Iraq.

Numerous times she'd considered telling him how she felt, but he'd never shown any interest outside of being her older brother's friend and her neighbor, and the thought of making him feel awkward… She'd just kept her feelings to herself. And as if she didn't have enough cards stacked against her, she'd heard from her brother Colton's views on combat troops who had to leave wives behind. He wasn't critical of the guys who were married but he would never think about marrying himself because he didn't want to put a woman in that position. Not when he stood a good chance of dying or coming back seriously injured.

Andi had replayed every snippet of their conversations, the little they'd exchanged on that visit, a thousand times. He'd been interested in and encouraged her in her college and career plans. He'd left and she'd prayed every day for his safe return. She'd told herself she had to get over him, that she was simply infatuated and she had no future with him.

She'd gone out of her way to make sure their paths didn't cross when he came back periodically to visit his mother and sister. She'd dated sporadically and then two years ago she'd met Blanton. They'd been engaged the past year. She'd *finally* gotten over Colton Sawyer. The irony that he'd be the one to step in for her brother in escorting her down the aisle and "giving her away" wasn't lost on her. Nonetheless, her heart was beating a little harder, a little faster, waiting on him to walk through the door.

"He's not going to make the rehearsal," Martha Anne said. "His flight was canceled due to storms. He won't be getting in until tomorrow morning but he should definitely make the wedding."

Disappointment warred with relief. She'd been waiting all afternoon to see him again for the first time in a long time, but now the proverbial moment of reckoning was put off a little longer.

Andi's mother, Daisy, shook her head, her salt-and-pepper bob swaying with the movement. "You'd have thought the army would've shown some understanding that this was Rion's sister's wedding and we needed him here." Andi knew how she felt. She'd been terribly disappointed her big brother wouldn't be sharing her big day with her. "It was sweet of Colton to step in for him." It was faint, but Andi didn't miss the grudging note. Her mother was careful to mask it but she resented Colton. Her attitude toward Colton had undergone a subtle change, but a change nonetheless, when Rion announced his decision to join the army. "But now he won't know what he's supposed to do tomorrow."

Sonya, their über-efficient wedding planner, made a soothing motion with her hands. "No problem. If he can arrive a few minutes early tomorrow I can easily go over with him what he needs to do. No worries." She smiled at the wedding party and the respective families. "We're done here. Tomorrow should go beautifully." She put her hands together and beamed. "It's going to be a day you'll never forget. Everyone can head over for the rehearsal dinner."

Blanton slipped his arm around Andi's waist and spoke up, "My last meal with my fiancée," he said, pulling her tighter against him. Everyone laughed except for Patrice, Andi's maid of honor. Andi wasn't altogether sure Patrice didn't have a bit of a thing for Blanton. Andi had caught a miserable expression on Patrice's face, one that reminded her of just how she'd felt when she'd been around Colton all those years ago, that made Andi wonder. Blanton continued, "I guess that didn't sound quite right. I just meant that when we have our next meal together, we'll be married." He really was a sweetie. He leaned in closer and murmured in her ear, "You might want to stick with just a salad tonight. You've put on a little weight." He tightened his hand on her waist for emphasis. "And I know you don't want to look chunky in the pictures tomorrow."

Well, there was nothing sweet about that. It was on the tip of her tongue to say if he didn't want to look like a jerk in the pictures tomorrow, he might want to just stay out of them since that was a butthead comment to make. However, she held her tongue.

This was the second time in a week he'd mentioned her weight. She'd planned to lose five pounds and she'd meant to really try but she'd been feeding her nerves for the past two weeks. She might've put on a pound or two that might've settled on her middle, but she'd be damned if she needed Blanton pointing it out to her. And she certainly didn't need him directing her food choices.

"Actually, I'm looking forward to the prime rib and mashed potatoes…along with the salad," she said sweetly. The words they'd just practiced echoed in her head: *for better, for worse, in sickness and in health.* She silently added her own verbiage, *and five pounds heavier.* "And cheesecake for dessert."

His look clearly said *I'm just trying to help,* but he wisely limited himself to an, "Okay."

Andi cut him some slack. He was probably as nervous about tomorrow as she was. She'd had some doubts in the past couple of weeks. She thought she and Blanton would have a good life together but she simply wasn't sure if it was enough. A very real part of her had always longed to leave Savannah and explore the world. She'd forever been drawn to Boston and New York, with San Francisco coming in a distant third.

Blanton had promised her they'd travel but then he'd balked on the honeymoon plans. Andi'd been thinking a bed-and-breakfast at one of California's wineries, she'd had her eye on one in Napa Valley. Blanton, however, had nixed going farther than the near-neighboring Sea Island for their honeymoon.

And perhaps he could be a little controlling at times and sometimes just a wee tad boring, but wasn't that what relationships were about? Compromise. And as her mother had told her when Andi had discussed her concerns with her, no one was perfect and if you loved someone, you worked through issues. So, who was to say Blanton wasn't suffering some of those same reservations she'd had?

Her father had named her Andromeda, which signified a maiden chained to a rock. Since the day her father died, and even more so once Rion left, her rock had been familial duty and obligation chained by love and guilt. Her mother wanted Andi close. It had been an ongoing mantra. And the looming threat of her mother having another breakdown had colored every decision Andi had made as a teenager and an adult.

She glanced at the man at her side. Her mother was thrilled Andi and Blanton were marrying. Andi knew that. Had it colored part of her decision to say yes? Perhaps, but she did love him. He had his faults like everyone else, the same as Andi had her faults, but she did love him, she reassured herself. Because if she didn't love him, that would be totally unfair to both of them, but particularly to him.

She linked her arm through his and offered him the sunniest smile she could muster. "Let's go eat. I'm starving."

"I HATE TO RUSH YOU, son, but we've got to get there a little early so the wedding planner can go over with you what you're supposed to do," his mother said as they walked in the door leading in from the garage to the kitchen.

She'd already told him twice in the car on the way from picking him up at the airport. Damn, just two hours later and he'd have been too late to make the wedding. As good as it was to be in the familiar house he'd grown up in with his grandmother's antique trunk against the den wall and all the family photographs spread throughout, he'd rather be back in Afghanistan than here.

His sister, Mattie, a little over a year younger than Colton, and back at home with their mother after her recent divorce, closed the door behind them. "I'm going to change," she said, excusing herself.

Mattie had been subdued, but he also knew from her emails that moving back home had been a difficult adjustment.

"You need the bathroom?" he asked.

"No, it's all yours," she said.

Colton nodded, heading across the den toward the stairs. "I'll hop in the shower then."

"Make sure you shave," his mother said.

She'd lobbed the same admonition his way since peach fuzz had appeared on his chin years ago. At thirty-two, Colton really didn't need to be reminded to shave. Nonetheless he gave the response she expected. "Yes, ma'am."

He started up the stairs to the landing that led to his and Mattie's bedrooms and a guest room that doubled as his mother's sewing room.

"We'll be ready to go in forty-five minutes," his mother said from the foot of the stairs. "You can ride with us."

Anyone who knew anything about Southern women realized that while the ideal was put forth that the men were in charge, it was actually the women who ran the show. Making the men *think* they were in charge was just part of the game. Until he died from a heart attack five years ago, Colton's father had been under that very misguided ideal. However, his mother didn't bother to even let Colton think he had a say-so in matters.

Hell no on this, however. He had his limits. "I'll go, but I'll drive the Buick." His father's sedan still sat in the garage. His mother took care of regular oil changes and tire rotations. Walking Andi down the aisle and then sitting through the wedding was one damn thing, but standing around a reception while she and her groom shoved cake in one another's mouths, toasted a long and happy future and then took to the dance floor together was another matter. Not only would Colton drive his own car, he'd make damn sure he wasn't blocked in and could hightail it out of there as soon as the I-do's had been exchanged.

Forty-five minutes later he followed his mother and Mattie down one of Savannah's numerous broad avenues overhung with oak trees draped in Spanish moss. After months in Afghanistan, he definitely appreciated Savannah's refined lushness of sprawling oaks, palms, verdant lawns and azaleas bursting with early-spring blooms.

How long did weddings typically last? Half an hour at the max? That's what he was counting on. He'd head home, change clothes and then mosey down to Ray-Ray's Bar and Grill where he could pick up a beer and a game of pool. His mother and Mattie would be tied up with the reception for hours afterward so they wouldn't even miss him.

His sister and mother pulled into the parking lot of the historic mansion that now served as a special-events location, primarily weddings. Architecture wasn't his thing so he didn't know if it was Italianate Renaissance or Greek Revival, but it was truly a mansion with a soaring facade that overlooked one of Savannah's more picturesque fountained squares. Colton supposed the house and grounds were nice enough for weddings and stuff, but the parking was a disaster area.

Not wanting to chance being blocked in, he circled the block and lucked out. A florist's van was just pulling away on the side street that offered access to the house through the side garden and rear parking area. He backed the Buick into the parallel parking spot.

He climbed out of the car and locked the door. All he had to do was make it through the next forty-five minutes then he was out of here, and Andi would be married to someone else.

2

"HOW ABOUT A mother-daughter photo here?" Marlena, the photographer, said, indicating Daisy and Andi should move away from the tufted ottoman in the dressing room. Marlena had been snapping candids left and right the entire time Andi, her bridesmaids and her maid of honor had their hair and makeup done and got dressed in the third-floor bridal suite.

The suite consisted of two elegantly appointed rooms with antique sofas, gilt-framed artwork, thick, fringed Oriental rugs over gleaming hardwood floors, and richly trimmed drapes framing the hundred-year-plus windows, plus an equally elegant tiled bathroom.

Marlena positioned them in front of the brocade-covered sofa. "Now, if you'll look at one another," she instructed.

Andi smiled at her mother, "You look great in that pink silk shantung, Mom."

"You just look beautiful, Andi," her mother said, tears glimmering in her eyes. Andi did rather feel like a princess. Her dress was truly lovely. It had been the first one she'd found when she went shopping. It suited her and the wedding setting.

It had an old-fashioned feel to it with a high collar in the back and a sweetheart neckline. The fitted bodice flared out into a full skirt with yards of tulle underlay. It was awkward as anything to get into and out of since, rather than a zipper, it buttoned all the way from the neck to the curve of her hips with small pearl buttons. It was equally awkward to sit with all the tulle layers but it was truly a beautiful dress, and she almost didn't recognize herself when she looked at her reflection.

The dress was spectacular, and Linda, the hairdresser, had artfully arranged her normally unruly red hair into an updo of curls. Diane, Linda's assistant, was equally genius with makeup. Out of nowhere the idea popped into Andi's head that Colton probably wouldn't recognize her if it weren't for the fact it could only be her in the wedding dress since it was her wedding. It was a silly thought and she turned her attention back to her mother.

Andi squeezed Daisy's hand. "Don't cry. Your makeup is perfect."

Daisy laughed. "There's no way I'm going to make it through this without boo-hooing anyway."

"Well, wait until you've been escorted down the

aisle and everyone sees how great you look," Andi said, determined to keep an upbeat note. She'd discovered at an early age the best way to keep her mother on an even keel was to keep things light and upbeat. And her mother on an even keel was definitely the desired outcome. Andi had spent the majority of her teenage and adult life avoiding another "episode" like her mother had had when Rion had left for college and the military.

"Perfect," Marlena said, snapping a rapid succession of shots. Beverly, the wedding planner's assistant, opened the door and stuck her head in. "Okay, ladies, it's time. I need the mother of the bride, the bridesmaids and the maid of honor downstairs now." She smiled brightly at Andi. "And you, ma'am, can come down in about ten minutes. We don't want any last-minute guests to see your gorgeous self yet and I understand your escort should be here momentarily so Sonya will need a few minutes to go over his duties with him."

Andi's stomach clenched and her pulse immediately accelerated. Colton was almost here. She felt breathless and anxious all at once, but then most brides probably felt this same way when they were ten to fifteen minutes away from strolling down the aisle. She pasted on a smile and hugged her mother, careful not to smear their makeup or damage their dresses. She squeezed the hands of her five friends and her cousin Emma as they left the room, sincerely telling each of them how beautiful they looked and how happy she was they were here to share this with her. The pale lavender, empire-waist gowns worked with everyone's complexion and body types. She'd gifted each of them with teardrop freshwater pearl-and-amethyst earrings she'd crafted herself.

And then the room was empty except for Andi and Marlena. Without the noise and general mayhem of everyone else around, butterflies erupted in her stomach and she began to sweat.

"Let's get a few shots of just you." Marlena led her over to one of the windows overlooking the side garden and street below. "Here, just look out the window, wait, tilt your head up just a tad, perfect. Look out and let your mind wander. If you feel pensive, that's fine, brides often are at this moment and it makes for lovely pictures."

Outside it was a flawless March day. White, fluffy clouds danced across an endless blue sky. Below, the trees swayed in the breeze. A movement on the sidewalk caught her eye. Colton, carriage erect, wearing his dress-blue uniform, entered the gate leading from the sidewalk to the garden. He closed it behind him and crossed the lawn, heading toward the front of the mansion.

Without warning or preface, the truth slammed into Andi with the force of a tsunami. She swayed on her feet and steadied herself with her hand to the windowsill. It wasn't as much a thought as it was a knowing that filled her. She hadn't gotten over Colton Sawyer—far from it.

She loved him. She was in love with him. She'd never felt one whit of what she felt looking at him now for Blanton. This wasn't a crush. This was love, soul-deep that wouldn't fade or go away with time. This was how she *should* feel about Blanton in order to take the vows she was about to. But the truth was undeniable—what she felt for Blanton didn't begin to touch what she felt for Colton.

Her mind whirled. She couldn't marry Blanton when she felt this way about another man. That simply wasn't fair to Blanton, or to her.

"Are you okay?" Marlena said, startling Andi. She'd forgotten the photographer was even there. "You look as if you've seen a ghost."

Andi mustered a smile. "I'm fine. But I'd like a minute or two alone, please. If you want to go on down, I'll be there shortly."

"Sure," Marlena said, but she looked hesitant. "Can I get you a glass of water or something before I go?"

She just wanted Marlena to leave so she could think uninterrupted, but Andi managed a weak laugh. "I don't dare drink in this dress. The bathroom isn't the easiest thing to manage."

Marlena grimaced. "I bet. Okay, I'll see you downstairs in just a minute." She closed the door behind her.

Finally. Andi was alone. What was she going to do? She couldn't in good faith go down there and promise to love Blanton till death do they part when she didn't, couldn't and wouldn't love him that way. She desperately needed to talk to someone, but all of her closest friends were downstairs waiting on her to make her appearance. A maelstrom of emotions rolled through her: guilt, elation, uncertainty over what to do, although there was no uncertainty regarding her feelings for Colton. She felt vulnerable and raw, but also, conversely, strong and empowered.

Think, Andi, think. But her only thought was she had to get out of here and now. She couldn't marry Blanton when she didn't love him and she felt too raw and open to face everyone or anyone. She rooted through her purse, pulling out her driver's license, credit card, debit card and the whopping ten-dollar bill she had in there. She stuffed the money and plastic in her bra under her left breast. Her cell phone and keys went inside her bra, under her right boob. If anyone looked closely she'd have one strange lump but she didn't plan on anyone getting that close to her.

Her heart thumping like mad, she opened the door and stepped out onto the landing. She eased the door closed behind her. To her left was a beautifully crafted mahogany staircase that wound down to the second floor and then the first. Forget that, she'd never make it down undetected, mainly because everyone would be standing down there waiting on her.

To her right, at the end of the hall was a vastly different stairway behind a closed doorway they'd been shown on the tour of the house. As Andi recalled it was narrow and plain, a servant's stairway. Heaven forbid that servants, or slaves, would've shared a staircase with guests or the master of the house.

Andi quickly made her way down the hall, making sure she tiptoed so as not to alert anyone with the clicking of her heels against the hardwood floor. She opened the door and paused. Holding on to the door frame, she pulled off her shoes. She'd never make it down the worn wooden stairs without making a ton of racket in her shoes.

Closing the door behind her, her knees shaking, she silently moved down the narrow stairs as quickly as she dared. If she tumbled down the stairs ass over end, that'd certainly cause a commotion, not to mention she'd probably wind up killing herself. And while she simply couldn't marry Blanton, she didn't want to kill herself either.

After what felt like a lifetime, she reached the bottom. Putting her shoes back on, she cracked the door open and peered out, getting her bearings. She faced the rear hall. The door to her left lead to the kitchen, the muted noise of the catering staff busy at work coming through. Leaving that way wouldn't work. First, she'd have everyone's attention, not to mention it would dump her out into the rear garden where a big white tent and linen-draped tables were ready for her reception. But the main reason it wouldn't work was because the Grand Ballroom where the ceremony was being held had floor-to-ceiling French doors that opened to the rear grounds, and the entire wedding ensemble would have a clear view of her hotfooting it out of there. Nix that option.

To the right the hall led to the foyer and the front door, where her attendants waited with the wedding planner…and Colton. Obviously that wouldn't work.

A rivulet of sweat trickled down her back and her armpits were soaking wet. She heard the flush of a toilet, the noise of water running in a sink and a door midway down the hall opened. One of Blanton's mother's friends from her garden club stepped out, pulling the door closed behind her. Bingo. A bathroom on ground level was exactly what she needed.

Remembering to tiptoe, she'd almost made it to the door when Marlena, her camera slung around her neck, spotted her. Silently, Andi made a face, pointed to the bathroom and did the dance universally recognized by women as the I've-got-to-pee jig. Marlena smiled and nodded in understanding.

Andi ducked into the bathroom and leaned against the door, her heart racing like a runaway train. Damn. Now instead of going upstairs to look for her, someone would be coming here in just a matter of minutes.

She had to act fast.

"You'll do just fine," the wedding planner said, patting his shoulder.

Colton nodded abruptly. "I've got it down."

He felt as if the walls were closing in on him. "I'm going to step outside for a minute. I need to make a call. I'll be back in—"

"Five minutes," Sonya finished for him, not giving him the opportunity to come up with his own timeline.

"Five minutes," he said, already heading for the front door. He just needed to step out into the fresh air and pull himself together. Jesus Christ, he was a major in the army. He was a soldier.

He stepped outside and rounded the corner of the house. He had five minutes to get his head into this. Operation Wedding Bells. He could do it. He'd undertaken far tougher assignments. The key was to disengage his emotions and where Andi was concerned that was damn hard.

Colton marched over to a small garden area that provided a little cover. He mentally reviewed all the reasons he'd never told her, or anyone else for that matter, how he felt about her. At the point he'd figured out how he felt, he was too old and she was too young. She was his best friend's sister and that would be damn awkward. Their mothers were best friends. Then, when she was older, he'd been about to ship out for his first deployment to Iraq and he strongly believed it was unfair to ask any woman to wait for him when he went to war. Bottom line, it simply wouldn't work.

He really needed an attitude adjustment but just couldn't seem to manage it. What had he thought? That Andi would simply sit around forever? For years she'd just been Rion's younger sister, six years their junior and usually a pain in the ass. And it wasn't as if he'd been slapped in the face one day with a realization that she'd grown into a beautiful woman. No, he'd seen her transition into a teenager and then a young woman as she graduated high school. She'd gone on to earn a degree and in the past few years she'd built an online business for her artisan, handcrafted jewelry.

Colton had been preparing for his first tour of duty in Iraq, sort of taking stock of his life, when he realized that on some level, Andi'd always been a part of his life and somewhere along the way had become an even more important part of him. But he was about to be embroiled in a war and how fair would that have been to her? Not to mention she'd never given him any indication she saw him as anything other than a surrogate older brother, plus the not-so-small matter that Daisy Mitchell would've probably hired a hit squad to take him out since his career would take him all over the world, but not Savannah, Georgia.

He checked his watch. It was time. Just as he was about to stand, a window on the side of the house, about midway, shot up. Andi stuck her head out of the window, her glance darting left and right. Heaven help him, but she was so beautiful his chest ached. The sun glinted off her red hair, the parts not covered by her white veil, picking out threads of gold and copper. She ducked back inside.

Colton surged to his feet and headed toward the open window. What was going on? Had she felt sick and needed fresh air? Did she need help?

He was halfway across the lawn when one shapely, hose-clad leg came through the window, then another, layers of white lace and dress and finally the rest of her.

She dropped to the ground, one of her heels sinking into the grass, throwing her off balance. As she began to fall backward, Colton automatically reached out and caught her.

"Whoa," he said.

Andi yelped in surprise.

For a second he allowed himself to absorb the feel of her in his arms—her scent, the press of her back and shoulders against his chest. Instinctively, he tightened his arms around her as if he could hold her close and never let her go.

She looked over her shoulder at him. "Colton?" Her cinnamon-brown eyes held specks of green and widened in surprise. He was a rational man, he always had been, but for a second he had the thoroughly irrational thought that her lips, with their gloss of red, begged for his kiss.

He released her before he did something totally

stupid like give in to the temptation to kiss her just before he walked her down the aisle. Or rather not walk her down the aisle, since she'd just scrambled out of a bathroom window.

"I think you're heading in the wrong direction," Colton said. "The wedding is that way."

Working her heel out of the lawn, she wouldn't look at him. "I know where the wedding is. I also know I'm not going to be part of it." Her foot free, she took both of her shoes off. "I can't talk to you now. I'm guessing I have about three, maybe four minutes before they come looking for me," she said, gathering up her dress and taking off at a jog across the grass, her veil flying out behind her.

Colton loped after her. "What's going on, Andi?"

She answered without looking at him, busy dodging an azalea loaded with bright pink blossoms. "I thought it was fairly obvious—I'm running away."

She stopped so suddenly he almost plowed into her. She tugged her shoes back on and he realized they were at the edge of a brick path leading to the rear parking lot. "I can see you're running away, but why?"

She hurried down the path, her heels clicking against the brick. He easily kept up with her. "I don't want to talk about it right now. I can't talk about it. But I can't marry Blanton."

"Can't or simply don't want to?" He couldn't

talk any sense into her if he didn't know what the problem was.

"Oh, no. No, no, no," she said with a slight wail. Before he could ask what, she said, "Mom's car is blocked in." Colton got it. She was counting on "borrowing" it, with the keys Daisy always left under the floor mats. From where they stood, they could hear the faint knocking on the bathroom door since the window was still standing open.

She looked at him. Near-panic—he'd seen the expression before in fellow soldiers—shadowed her eyes. "I think I'm down to about two, possibly three minutes. I know you're parked on the street. I need to borrow your car."

"Andi, I don't think—"

"Please, Colton. I can't go in there right now and face all of them. I just need to get away. Rion would help me if he was here." This was true. "Please, Pyxis," she said, falling back on the name she'd called him growing up. "I promise I'll return the car."

He scrubbed his hand over his head. The sounds of someone entering the bathroom and calling Andi's name floated across the lawn. The photographer stuck her head out the window. The wedding planner's head popped up over her shoulder. Andi ducked like someone being sighted in a sniper's crosshairs.

"Sweet mercy," one of the women said, her voice carrying clearly across the way. "She's left."

They disappeared back inside the window. "They're gone," he said.

Still crouching she started across the back parking area. "What are you doing?"

"Leaving. If you won't give me the keys then I'll start walking and call a cab." She reached inside the bodice of her dress and pulled out her cell phone.

She was totally serious and totally determined. He made a decision. At least if he was with her, he could take care of her. "Come on," he said, taking her by the arm. "I'm not giving you the key when you're upset and you can't drive in that dress anyway. I'll take you wherever it is you want to go."

The way he saw it, driving her getaway car was a damn sight better than handing her off to marry Blanton.

3

ANDI JUMPED INTO THE passenger seat, pulled the wad of tulle and material inside the car and slammed the door shut. Her skirt was so full she could barely see out. Colton was right. Driving would've been difficult, but where there was a will there was a way. She'd have made it work.

He already had the car in Drive and was pulling out into the street. "That dress is a road hazard," he said as he nearly sideswiped a car that he hadn't seen on account of her mountain of fabric.

"This dress is a *life* hazard," she said without thinking. She'd come so close to making such a big mistake. And now the reality of what she'd done and who she was with sank in. She hadn't been ready to face Blanton quite yet, but she also hadn't been ready to face Colton either. But here she was in the close, intimate confines of the car and it was as if she was a sponge absorbing his nearness.

She hadn't seen him in so long and she looked at him now, making sure to mask the hunger in her eyes. The midafternoon sun slanted into the car. Lines that hadn't been there the last time she saw him radiated from his eyes and bracketed his mouth. She longed to reach over and trace them with her finger. She didn't know if it was the harsh landscape of Afghanistan, the trials of war or more likely a combination of the two but he looked older, more seasoned. All traces of the boy she'd grown up with were gone and he'd become the man she'd denied in her heart for so long. And there was a whole lot more than just her heart engaged. Desire and longing tightened her body and quickened her breath. The need to touch him was nearly overwhelming. Desperate, she mentally scrambled for something to say before she blurted something absolutely off the chart like, *I love you* or *I want you*. The only thing her whirling brain and tilting hormones could come up with was, "So, how have you been?"

He looked at her as if she'd lost her mind and she wasn't altogether too sure she hadn't. Actually, she could only imagine the look on his face if she'd blurted out how she felt about him. "Fine. I'm still in one piece. Now where am I taking you? Your house? Your apartment?"

Inside her bodice, her phone rang. Checking caller ID, she shook her head. "It's my mother. I'm not answering. I'm not ready to talk to her." Part of her wished she'd managed to escape on her own because the realization she'd just come to was too fresh and she needed some time alone to work through her emotions. But another part of her was crazy happy just to be with Colton in the here and now, even if she had just run out on her own wedding.

Her emotions were all whacked-out. She felt horrible because she knew Blanton would never understand that she'd walked out because to do otherwise wasn't fair. She might not feel about him the way she felt about the man sitting next to her, but she certainly didn't want to hurt Blanton—and leaving him at the altar wasn't nearly as hurtful in her book as marrying him when she loved someone else.

But she just couldn't deal with her mother right now. She pushed the button, sending the call to voice mail. However, she did send a quick text message telling her mother she was fine and would call in a bit, otherwise Daisy would be frantic that Andi had simply disappeared.

The impact of what she'd just done hit her. How many people were going to be furious with her? And this would feed the gossip coffers for more than a little bit. A faint nausea roiled through her but in her heart she knew she'd done the right thing. And everything happened for a reason. If Marlena hadn't wanted her at that window…if Colton hadn't been arriving right at that time…if she hadn't seen him and realized she was in love with him, she would've made one of the biggest mistakes of her life. Instead, she was sitting next to Colton now. She glanced over at his profile simply because she could. He would be leaving in less than a week.

He returned her look. "Andi, where am I taking you?" Colton said, breaking the silence.

She didn't know. She hadn't thought about it. Her single objective had been to get away from the wedding, to find some breathing room. "I gave up my apartment and moved everything to Mom's house. I've been staying with her until the wedding, but we ran my car over to Blanton's last night after the rehearsal dinner." She rubbed at her forehead, a headache beginning to form like storm clouds gathering on the horizon. "Do you think we could just drive for a while until I can figure out what to do?" The sun slanting through the windshield warmed her. For the first time in what felt like forever she didn't have the tremendous weight of the impending wedding bearing down on her. True enough, now she had to deal with being a runaway bride, but it was certainly the better of the two choices.

She couldn't shuck the dress as she had nothing to change into, but she could lose the veil. She loosened the cap holding the lace and tulle in place and tossed it into the backseat. That felt better. "I know my mother. She'll send someone to Blanton's place and someone to her house."

Colton made a left. "Andi, don't you think it'd

just be better to face the music now? I'll have your back."

"You'll have my back?" she repeated. "But you don't even know why I'm running away."

"It doesn't matter," he said simply. "I'll still have your back."

She looked at his strong jaw, at his hands steady on the wheel. He wasn't a man to say things like that lightly. Something sweet and simple turned over inside her as she acknowledged Colton was solid—a man you could count on through thick and thin. This was why she was stuck on Colton Sawyer.

"That is one of the sweetest things anyone has ever said to me." She went with her need to touch him and reached over, placing her hand on his arm. He tensed at her touch. Even through the layers of his shirt and jacket the bunching of his biceps beneath her fingers and palm sent a quiver through her. "Unconditional backing isn't exactly a commodity in our household, as you well know." His nod bordered on curt and she removed her hand. "And I appreciate it, but do you think we could just drive for a while?"

"Sure." The lines bracketing his eyes crinkled with his smile, and in that instant, there was a shift between them, a connection, strong and intense and so charged with sexual energy the air seemed to sizzle between them. "Wherever you want to go." There was no mistaking the husky note in his voice.

Wherever you want to go. Her initial, impractical

thought was she wanted to go nowhere in particular and everywhere, just as long as she could be with him, just the two of them, until he had to leave again. And that foolish notion wasn't at all what he'd meant. They stopped at a traffic light and the couple in the car next to them stared. They'd get that reaction all day driving around town. She made a snap decision. "Let's hit the expressway. Too many people are going to be looking if we're driving around town with this wedding dress filling up the front seat."

"The expressway it is," he said.

As they drove in silence, Andi stared sightlessly out of the window. Instead of the spring day, she merely saw the numerous gifts in her mother's living room, waiting to be returned now that the wedding was called off. And she saw Colton leaving Savannah once again to report for duty in five days. The presents she could deal with, but his leaving...

Colton was entering I-95 south when he pulled out his cell phone. "My mother," he said, reading the display. He'd obviously had it on vibrate. "Might as well get this out of the way." He hit the on button. "What's up, Mom?"

"Don't you 'what's up, Mom' me." It didn't matter that he didn't have the speakerphone on. Martha Anne Sawyer's voice was clearly audible to Andi. "Is Andi with you?"

"Yes, ma'am, she is."

"Oh, Lord, Lola Bridgerton was right." Andi

winced. Lola was only the biggest gossip in Savannah. Now not only would the story be that Andi had ditched Blanton at the altar, the equally juicy part would be that she'd left with Colton Sawyer. "You turn right around and bring her back. She's supposed to be getting married."

Andi kept her mouth shut but shook her head no. Her head swam dizzily—maybe because she hadn't eaten since the rehearsal dinner last night when she'd actually only picked at her plate despite her and Blanton's postrehearsal conversation.

"No can do, Mom. She doesn't want to get married today."

"Why not?"

"I don't know that answer yet, but she doesn't."

Andi could've kissed him for that. Actually, she'd happily kiss him for no good reason other than because he was sexy and she wanted him, but she could still kiss him for his solid backing nonetheless.

"Son, bring her back. Everyone's still here. Every bride gets cold feet. Just tell her to come on back and no harm, no foul. It'll make a good story for them to tell their children one day."

No, because she was not going to have children with Blanton because she was not marrying him. Andi shook her head and said to Colton, "I'm not going back. Will you tell your mom that everyone should go home and I'm so sorry for the inconvenience?" Actually, she didn't know how that worked—did people simply stay and go ahead and hang out at the reception since the food and facility were already paid for? Sonya, the wedding planner, would know those things.

"That's not going to work out for Andi. She says everyone should just go home."

"Colton, turn that car around." Martha Anne's voice had escalated.

"Not going to happen. Look, I've got to run but I'll check in with you later. And tell Ms. Daisy not to worry. I'll take care of Andi."

Colton ended the call as his mother started to say something.

"Hanging up was a smart move," Andi said. "She'd argue with you all day to do her bidding if you didn't just cut her off. And I can say that because she's as relentless as my mother, which is probably why they're such good friends."

Andi reached over and touched his arm again. She couldn't seem to help herself. Although his expression didn't change, he tensed once again and she realized it wasn't because he didn't like her touching him, it was because he did like it. She could practically feel his sexual energy in a way she'd never experienced with anyone else. "Thanks. I owe you."

"You don't *owe* me anything," he said, putting on his blinker and smoothly changing lanes. "But I wouldn't mind an explanation."

She owed him that, and it wasn't as if she wouldn't

be fielding this topic for the next several weeks. She figured there was no substitute for the truth…or at least a portion of it. "I'm going to be doing a lot of explaining when I go back so I might as well practice on you."

HE SWORE HE COULD STILL feel the heat of her touch against his arm. Being with her like this was a sweet torture. It was as if all his senses were heightened by an adrenaline rush, as if he was more tuned in to himself and to her. One simple touch, one curve of her lips and his desire for her, what was damn near a *need* for her, knotted harder and tighter inside him.

He forced himself to focus on another need. Colton needed to know why she'd felt so desperate she'd climbed out of a bathroom window. He just hoped it wasn't a matter of Blanton having ever struck her or cheated on her because then he'd have to seriously hurt the son of a bitch…and Rion would be right in line behind Colton. He set the car on cruise control, the traffic on the expressway extremely light.

The silence stretched between them and he could swear she was as aware of him as a man as he was conscious of the curve of her breasts against the neckline of her dress. "I'm ready when you are," he said. He'd meant for her explanation but it seemed to take on a whole different meaning and the air seemed to thicken even more between them.

"Well," she said, knotting her fingers together. "The bottom line is I don't love him."

She didn't love him? She didn't love him. Rion had guessed as much and a part of Colton foolishly rejoiced at the news. But it still didn't give him the right, or rather make it right for him to do what he wanted to do, which was pull the car over and kiss her tempting lips and then work his way down the length of her neck to the sweet valley between her breasts.

Colton sensed there was something else, something she was holding back. He hadn't seen her in years but there was a part of him that knew her on a level he couldn't explain. "That's it?"

"Don't you think that's enough?" Her voice raised a notch, a telling mix of panic wrapped in defensiveness. She was definitely hiding something.

"That's plenty," he said, backpedaling hard. "You should love him if you marry him." He still wanted the bigger questions answered. There were numerous reasons she could've decided she didn't love Blanton after agreeing to marry him. Andi had always been free-spirited and fun, but she had also been very responsible. For her to decide she didn't love the man at the eleventh hour—that realization had to be driven by something cataclysmic for her to walk out on her wedding. "But he never hit you or ran around on you?"

Genuine surprise registered on her face. "Good God, no."

Colton nodded, satisfied. "Well, that's good. That

means he gets to live another day or at least he won't wind up in the hospital."

"You're serious, aren't you?" A faint note of awe colored her voice.

What kind of men had she grown used to since he and Rion had left? No man worth a damn would put up with anyone treating her that way. "Take it to the bank."

"Come on," Andi said. From the corner of his eye he saw her wrinkle her nose, one of those quirky things she'd done for as long as he could remember. "You know I'd never put up with something like that."

No, he couldn't imagine it of the girl and young woman he'd known. He distinctly remembered when she was nine and he and Rion were fifteen, Andi had been sent home from school for fighting. She'd taken on a kid twice her size who made it a habit to bully kids half her size. All she'd needed to do was apologize to the bully. Even at nine, she'd stood firm on her principle and taken a three-day suspension instead. So, no, the Andi of old would've never tolerated infidelity or abuse, but people changed.

Quite frankly, he would've never imagined her leaving a groom, several hundred guests and, most importantly, her mother. "Let me remind you, you did just climb out of a bathroom window to get out of marrying him."

"Hel-lo. That's because he's boring and I don't love

him. Everyone kept telling me what a great couple we made and what a great catch he was and I bought into it."

He wasn't buying into it. Blanton probably was boring and maybe she didn't love the guy, but there was more to it than she was telling. Nonetheless, he simply said, "Okay." He wasn't going to push her. She'd tell him the rest if and when she wanted him to know.

She leaned her head back against the headrest, as if she was suddenly exhausted. "You know, Colton, I've always tried to be a dutiful daughter but I realized today I had to draw the line at marrying someone I didn't love, even if that's what my mother wants."

"Do you really think your mother would want you to marry someone you didn't love?"

"I tried to talk to her about it." Andi wrapped her arms around her middle. "I told her I didn't know if I really loved him and she assured me it was okay, that even if I didn't, I'd grow to love him. But I'm just not seeing that happen."

"That answered that question."

"She's never going to forgive me for this."

Ms. Daisy was a different animal altogether. "It'll take some time, but she will."

Andi raised a skeptical eyebrow in his direction.

"Okay, well, maybe a lot of time. She still hasn't forgiven me for Rion joining the military." He finally voiced what he'd thought for a long time. "Even though I didn't have anything to do with it. I just knew it was what I wanted to do."

"No, she hasn't," Andi said, confirming his suspicion. Colton had mentioned it to Rion once and in typical Rion fashion he'd just blown it off. "This isn't going to exactly redeem you."

Colton shrugged. He was aware of both. "Might as well be hung for a lamb as a sheep."

"What?" Andi adopted a teasing tone. "This from the guy who never got into trouble? Who always does the right thing, even when the right thing isn't the easy thing to do? Mr. Dependable?"

Is that how she saw him? Well, obviously it was. Damnation but he sounded boring as hell, too; however, he was what he was. "That's Major Dependable, if you would. And maybe I think helping you now is the right thing to do." He would go to the ends of the earth if it was what she needed. Hell, he'd gone to the ends of the earth to stay away from her because he'd thought that was exactly what she needed.

Her smile turned him inside out. Andi had always had a way of smiling… It was sort of impish, as if she was including you in something very special, something a little forbidden, or perhaps it was simply because she had always been forbidden. "Well, we both know there's going to be some differing opinions on whether helping me run out on my wedding was the right thing to do."

"I'm a big boy, I think I can handle it."

"I'm sure glad you feel that way. I tell you what you could do to help right now."

"And this would be in addition to driving your getaway car?"

"Yep." Her grin was unrepentant for dragging him into her shenanigans. "I'm starving. I was too nervous to eat this morning. Actually, I was downright nauseous. I didn't have breakfast or lunch but now that I've flown the coop, I'm ravenous."

So was he, but his hunger was a different one altogether. What she was talking about was far easier and far safer to accommodate. There was no end to fast-food restaurants along interstate stretches. "What do you want?"

For a second he had the insane idea her eyes had flashed *you* at him. Being with Andi had him totally off his usual well-reasoned track.

"Breakfast," she said.

Okay, that wasn't easy enough. "Can we aim for a burger or something considering it's mid-afternoon?"

She was already shaking her head no. "Waffle House. I want eggs, smothered, covered, chunked, peppered hash browns and a pecan waffle." She pointed to the roadside sign. "See, next exit. One and a half miles."

"That's great, but you're going to go into the Waffle House wearing a wedding dress?"

"Absolutely. I'm so hungry I'm ready to gnaw my own hand off."

This was about to be weird and awkward, but what the hell, the whole day had been weird and awkward already. He put on his blinker and slowed for the exit. "Then let's save your hand and feed you now."

4

ANDI COULDN'T SEE PAST all of her wedding-dress material to locate the door handle in Colton's car. The layers of tulle underskirt poofed out the dress so it looked as if she actually had a waistline. But it definitely lent itself more to standing than sitting. She pushed aside a mass.

"Just hang tight and I'll come around and get you out," he said, shaking his head and laughing.

"Okay." She settled back against the seat and waited as he rounded the car to open the door. It was true Rion would've helped her get away from the wedding but she was glad it had been Colton for a number of reasons—primarily because she wanted to be with him, but the other bottom line was Rion wasn't nearly as thoughtful and accommodating as Colton. If Rion hadn't wanted Waffle House, he'd have told her to get over herself and pulled into whatever fast-food drive-through *he* wanted. And he darn sure wouldn't be coming around opening her door for her. She laughed at the thought.

Colton opened the door and cool March air flooded the car. "What's so funny?"

"I was just thinking how glad I am it's you instead of Rion here. He wouldn't open the door for me and if he hadn't wanted to go to Waffle House, we wouldn't be here, we'd be eating where he wanted to eat."

Colton smiled. "That's Rion, for sure." He held out his hand. "Here, I'll help you out."

Placing her palm in his, he wrapped his fingers around her hand and tugged her upward. A tingle shot through her and Andi felt dizzy. Her entire balance was thrown off as she levered too fast and too hard to her feet. She landed against the broad wall of his chest with a *thunk*. Immediately his other arm shot around her, wrapping around her waist to steady her.

She braced her other hand against his chest and a sudden breathlessness washed over her. She wasn't sure if she'd ever been this close to Colton as an adult. Andi looked up and everything else around them seemed to vanish. She lost herself in his green eyes for what could have been seconds or a lifetime. On one hand she knew an abiding contentedness, a desire to stay there forever, but on the other hand she wanted much, much more. She wanted to link her arms about his neck and press herself more firmly, more intimately against his lean strength. Instinctively, she did press closer to him.

"You okay?" he asked. His breath, warm and fragrant, stirred against the curling tendril the hairdresser had draped over Andi's left temple when she'd given Andi her updo.

"I'm fine." Other than her nearly debilitating desire for him. "I'm just a little light-headed from not eating and I lost my balance." That much was true. She left off the part about wanting him desperately.

"Then we'll definitely get you inside and fed." He released her hand but kept his arm firmly around her waist.

"I'm fine now," she said but made absolutely no attempt to move away from him. She liked his nearness, the feel of his solid warmth next to her and his clean scent.

"I'm not taking any chances with you face-planting on the sidewalk," he said as they stepped onto the sidewalk from the parking lot.

She elbowed him in the side. "That makes me feel elegant."

He grinned down at her and something warm and wonderful shot through her. "I can't help that but I can keep you from falling while you're on my watch."

"Ah, the sacrifices of a man with honor."

"You have no idea," he murmured somewhat cryptically as he pushed open the restaurant door and then the one beyond that.

The moment they crossed the threshold, clapping and whooping erupted. Andi was startled. She'd been so wrapped up in Colton she hadn't even thought about the people inside the restaurant.

"Welcome to Waffle House," said one of the waitresses behind the counter in standard Waffle House greeting. She was an older woman with short dark hair. Everyone else beamed at Colton and Andi, including the guy manning the grill.

The greeter continued, "When you helped her out of that car and swept her up close to you and then y'all stood there gazing into one another's eyes—that was the most romantic thing I've ever seen. Wait." She threw up her hand. "We've never had newlyweds come in still all dressed up." She dabbed at her eyes with a paper napkin. "I'm sorry…I always cry at weddings. And seeing the two of you gazing into one another's eyes in the parking lot just did my heart a world of good. I've got one request, though."

"Actually—" Colton said.

Andi dug her elbow into his side, cutting him off. He was about to spill the beans but she was all for having them mistaken as a couple. Perhaps it would plant a seed in his practical brain. "Honey, she has a request."

The woman clasped her hands together. "Would you just back up and carry her across our threshold?"

"But…" Colton began.

"Sure he can," Andi cut him off again. "Can't you, darling?"

His hand tightened where it still rested on her waist. "No problem, honey bunny."

They backed out of the door. The moment it closed behind them, he looked down at her. "Andi, I'm just curious. Is there some particular reason we're pretending to be happy newlyweds?"

She thought it best not to tell him she wanted him to embrace the notion of the two of them as an item through the power of suggestion. She rolled with the other reason. It was called saving face. "It just seems easier. First off, she was so happy for us, they all were."

"But there is no *us*."

"I know that and you know that." And she was going to do her damnedest to change that starting right now. "But if they know that they'll be disappointed. Plus, if we tell them I buggered out on the wedding—well, I already look like a flake in front of half of Savannah." That was certainly no lie. "I just don't want to look like a flake again."

For a second she thought he might balk but he simply sighed. "Then let's do this thing."

Wrapping one arm behind her back, he swept the other arm beneath her knees and scooped her up. Instinctively, she linked her hands behind his neck, her fingers grazing against the short hair on the back of his head. He grinned down at her. "Hope I don't get some kind of back strain."

"You'll pay for that crack, Major," she managed

to quip, but her heart was thumping in her chest like nobody's business at being held so close.

He pushed through the door and once again, the smattering of customers and the staff all broke into applause. Colton set her back on her feet and she reluctantly unlinked her hands from around his neck.

The waitress who'd orchestrated the threshold deal, Rochelle according to her name tag, swiped at her eyes again. "I just can't help the waterworks. Y'all sit anywhere you want to but if you choose one of those booths," she said, waving her hand to the right, "that's my section."

"How about that one?" Andi said, nodding toward one in Rochelle's area because she obviously wanted to serve them.

"Works for me," Colton said, ushering her that way with a light hand to the small of her back. She had to wonder if he didn't want to touch her just as much as she wanted to touch him. She was thinking that might be the case.

Andi had so much dress going on they had to settle into a booth for four and it was still something of a squeeze getting in there.

Rochelle came over as soon as Colton settled opposite her. Mercifully, everyone else went back to doing what they'd been doing before. It was a little disconcerting being the center of that kind of attention.

"Do y'all know what you want or do you need a few minutes?"

Colton grinned. "Oh, she knows exactly what she wants."

Her newly claimed heart recognized she could happily look at that grin every day for the rest of her life. But back to the matter at hand, namely food… Andi repeated the same rundown she'd given Colton in the car. "Oh, yeah, and a side of sliced tomatoes. And sweet tea." She'd been hungry before but she was suddenly so ravenous she couldn't think straight.

"Honey, are you already eating for two?" Rochelle said. She turned to Colton and winked. "You rascal, you."

Andi laughed aloud at the look on his face but she couldn't deny the feeling inside her at the thought of having been his lover and actually being pregnant.

"She's just hungry," Colton said, giving her a quelling look. She watched him consideringly across the table as he placed his order.

Colton was far, far too responsible to get a girl knocked up prewedding. Not that she didn't think he had sex, but he'd just make darn sure everyone was protected because that's the kind of guy he was and a woman had to admire that in a man. However, she didn't want to think of him with another woman. The very idea made her queasy.

How had he managed to dodge the marriage bullet for so long? Well, her brother had as well but Rion wasn't the prize Colton was, even if he was her brother.

"Behave," Colton said across the table with a quirky smile as Rochelle sang out their order.

"I'll try to behave but as Rion would say, I'm up to my ass in alligators with a whole bunch of people," Andi said. "So I might as well have fun while I still can." And especially while she was with him. "It sure isn't going to be anything but miserable when you take me back." She pushed aside the thought. "And I'm not even going to think about it and ruin my meal."

Rochelle returned with their drinks, placing them on the table. She peered at Andi's left hand. "Honey, that's some ring, there." Andi had gotten so used to wearing it she'd forgotten all about having it on. Rochelle nodded approvingly at Colton. "You did good."

"Thanks," he murmured.

Andi liked watching him squirm. It was good to have Rochelle forcing Colton to see Andi in a different light. If that look in his eyes was anything to go by earlier, he was seeing her in a different light than simply Rion's pain-in-the-butt younger sister.

"Where y'all heading on your honeymoon?" Rochelle asked, obviously in no hurry to leave their table.

"Jekyll Island," Andi said off the top of her head.

"Orlando," Colton said at the same time.

"Surprise, honey," Andi said. "Change of plans."

Rochelle cocked her head to one side and eyed them for what felt like forever. "My husband's always telling me I mind business that isn't mine to mind, so feel free to do the same, but are y'all really married or are you a bride on the lam?"

Well, so much for going with the newlywed cover. But Andi was curious as to what gave them away unless it was just the honeymoon mix-up. "What makes you say that?"

"Well, I love all those detective shows. Now when y'all first drove up, I just took everything at face value, your dress, his uniform, the way y'all were looking at one another in the parking lot. But then I got to noticing things. You didn't go to see a justice of the peace wearing that dress. That's a dress you wear for a big fancy wedding. And folks always decorate the car at a big fancy wedding, but your car isn't decorated. And you might leave your reception in your wedding dress but it's usually not to go to a Waffle House to eat. He's not wearing a ring and lots of men don't wear rings but if you just tied the knot, he'd still have his on. And last but not least is the way the two of you look at one another. When one of you thinks the other one's not looking, you look at the other one the way someone just married would, but not when the other one is looking. And if I'm way off base, I apologize."

Across the booth, Colton looked at Andi and shrugged. "I guess we weren't meant to be married, even pretend." Andi pasted on a smile but his words made her want to grind her teeth. There was the power of suggestion and then, better yet, there was definitive action.

If there was one thing she'd learned today it was she had to make something happen with Colton Sawyer. They were going to either have something together or she'd get him out of her system and then she could move on. But one way or the other, she was going to have him. The time for denial was done. Denial had led her to climbing out a bathroom window at her own wedding.

Time to formulate a Plan B.

THERE WAS A PART OF him that simply had to put an end to the newlywed fantasy in words—mainly because it was all too tempting to get caught up in the pretense she was his. Even though he'd long known how he felt about her, he'd never allowed himself to think in terms of her being his.

Andi looked away from him and squarely faced Rochelle. "Yes, I am a runaway bride. I let you think we were newlyweds because it's embarrassing to admit I didn't figure something out until the last, and I mean *last,* minute."

Rochelle patted Andi on the shoulder and clucked sympathetically. "Honey, I don't know what you walked out on, but this here is one fine man." She jerked her head in Colton's direction. "And a soldier to boot. Ain't nobody gonna blame you for picking him." Andi opened her mouth but Rochelle just kept talking, turning her attention to Colton. "You home on leave or you stationed at Ft. Hunter or Ft. Stewart?"

"I'm home on leave from Afghanistan but my home base is in Massachusetts." Damn, he had to set this straight all over again. "I didn't sweep anyone anywhere. All I did was show up for the wedding. I was supposed to give her away."

Rochelle smiled brighter than before. "What was it, hon?" she said to Andi. "One look at him and you knew you were making a mistake?"

Colton had always prided himself on being a man of logic. However, now he found himself holding an illogical breath that she might say yes, even though she hadn't technically seen him until she'd climbed out the window and even though she hadn't given him a remote inkling he had a thing to do with her decision to run—and it wouldn't matter if he had. They would always be at the impasse of his career and her family.

"Colton—" Andi pointed toward him "—he's Colton and I'm Andi—was supposed to give me away." Andi ran through the situation with Rion's denied leave and how Colton wound up in the position of escorting her down the aisle on behalf of her family. "Anyway, Colton didn't come in and sweep me away. I climbed out of a bathroom window. When I hit the ground, he was there."

"What were you doing outside the bathroom window?" Rochelle said to Colton.

That almost made him sound like some pervert. "I'd stepped outside for a minute before the ceremony," he said.

"Ah," Rochelle said, nodding with understanding. "A matter of being in the right place at the right time."

Or wrong place at the wrong time. "Something like that," Colton said.

"I see," Rochelle said, looking closely from him to Andi and back to him. For all that she'd gotten so much supposition wrong, Colton had the weirdest sense that Rochelle did, in fact, see more than he'd like. She finally looked back at Andi. "So, why'd you climb out the window?"

"Rochelle, order up!" the guy behind the grill yelled.

She held up a staying finger. "Hold that thought and I'll be right back with your food."

As Rochelle headed to the kitchen to pick up their order, Andi scrutinized him across the table. She'd always been quick and a sharp intelligence gleamed in her eyes. "Why weren't you inside? The wedding was about to start and I thought you were reviewing your part with Sonya."

Because I needed a minute outside—because I was about to do something that was even harder than going into combat. "I told you both, I was heading that way."

"Yeah, but—"

Rochelle returned with their plates, shutting Andi's interrogation down. "Here ya go. I know you're hungry, hon, so I don't mind if you talk and eat at the same time," she said to Andi. "You were about to tell me why you climbed out that window." She settled next to their table, one hand on her hip.

While they ate, Andi relayed the same thing she'd essentially told him in the car. Rochelle crossed her arms over her chest, shaking her head. "Nope, you can't marry a man you don't love. It's hard enough to live with 'em when you love 'em. Isn't that right, Vern?" She yelled the last part to the cook.

"Whatever you say, Rochelle, darlin'," Vern returned with an indulgent eye roll.

"He's my old man," she said to them with a wink. "We've been together thirty years now. He's the best thing that ever happened to me." She eyeballed the two of them. "I don't believe in coincidence. You were supposed to climb out that window," she said to Andi. "And you were supposed to be there." She directed the last part to Colton. "Now the rest is up to you to figure out." She winked. "Guess I better get back to work, huh? Y'all need anything else right now?"

Colton looked at Andi, who shook her head. "We're fine," he said.

"She's nice," Andi said, just before she shoved a forkful of pecan waffle into her lovely mouth.

He was like a man who'd been stumbling through the desert for years and had finally found an oasis.

He couldn't seem to get enough of looking at her—the sweep of her lashes, the curve of her cheek, the graceful lines of her neck, the slope of her breasts. The urge to touch her was a physical ache inside him. It was one thing to deny himself when she was half a world away. He was discovering it wasn't nearly as damn easy when there was just a table between them.

Colton cut into his eggs. "I don't know that I particularly buy into her lack of coincidence theory, but yeah, she was nice."

Andi pointed her fork at him as she finished chewing. She swallowed. "Maybe she's on to something. If you had been anyone else, I'd have been stuck but your car was in a good place and you were willing to help me out." She smiled and there was a gleam in her eyes that told him loud and clear she was very much aware he was a man and she was a woman. The room suddenly felt ten degrees warmer. "I think you *were* meant to be there. We were obviously meant to be here," she said, grinning, "because I'm finally feeling human again with some food in me." She rounded up a forkful of hash browns.

"Oh, is that the barometer?"

"It's as good as any." She grew serious. "Thank you, Colton. I don't know what I would've done without you. And I know your mom isn't happy with you."

True enough, Martha Anne wouldn't be happy but she'd get over it. "I'm a big boy. I can handle it."

"Well, you're my hero."

The look in her eyes made him hot. It was a damn good thing the table was between them and there were other people around because otherwise he wasn't so sure he could've stopped himself from pulling her tight and hard against him and kissing her. They were wandering into territory where they didn't belong. "Thanks."

Her smile knotted his gut. "I've got an idea."

"That sounds dangerous." She was dangerous.

"Ha, ha. Very funny. You know we're both going to be in trouble—me for taking off and you for taking me."

"Yes?"

"Well, I'm going to hear about it from my family and you're going to hear about it from yours…"

She had all of that right so far, but self-preservation made him wary of where she was taking this. "Uh-huh. Nonstop, until I head back."

"Let's don't go back yet. I planned for the week off and you're on leave. Let's have a Grand Adventure."

He was shaking his head before she finished talking. "Bad idea."

"Why?"

Because how the hell was he supposed to spend nearly a week with her and continue to resist temptation? He'd jumped on every reasonable excuse to touch her earlier. "Because…well, it just is."

"Did you have any plans for the week? If you were going to look up Diane Lassiter, she got married last year."

Where had Andi come up with the notion he'd look up this old Senior Prom date? "I know Diane got married last year. She friended me on Facebook. No, I don't have any particular plans." He found he couldn't lie to her about it. "But taking off on a Grand Adventure isn't a good idea." And that was an understatement. It had *disaster* written all over it.

"You're right, it's not a good idea." Thank God she was going to be reasonable about this. "It's a *great* idea. You're the one who said you might as well be hung for a sheep as for a lamb. It'll be fun." She gave him that beseeching look that had always worked when they were younger. "C'mon. Pretty please."

He wasn't going to be swayed by her. "No."

"Suit yourself, but I am not going back and I'm going to have my adventure. I've got a credit card." She looked at him across the table with cool defiance. "Just drop me off at a rental-car company and I'll take it from there."

Dammit to hell. "You're serious?"

"One hundred percent. You and Rion have been off doing what you wanted to do, where you wanted to do it." He leveled a let's-get-real look at her. "Okay, so maybe Afghanistan isn't your first choice of places to be, but you're not sitting around in Savannah being the dutiful daughter." She leaned across the table and reached for him, placing her hand on top of his, her fingers warm and smooth against his. He quite literally couldn't think straight when she touched him, even just her hand on his. "You know how my mother is. She's going to be livid." No shit. "So I might as well have some fun before I go back since I've already sunk my ship, so to speak." She moved her hand to rim her tea glass with her index finger.

Colton knew that obstinate set of her chin. She was serious. She wasn't going back…at least not today. She was hell bent for leather that she'd have her—how'd she put it—Grand Adventure. He couldn't stop her, he knew Andi well enough to know that, but he could make sure she didn't get into trouble and that she was okay. And there was only one way to do that. "Okay. Fine."

"Fine what? I wasn't asking your permission to go."

"I didn't think you were." He knew her better than that.

She paused in toying with her glass. "Then what's fine?"

He was so going to regret this. Hell, he already regretted it. "I'll go with you."

"For real?" A huge smile blossomed on her face and lit her eyes.

He was sunk, he was in way too deep because just

the idea that he'd been the one to light up her eyes like that made him feel ten feet tall, made him want to scale mountains and whatever else was necessary to get that response. "For real."

She rubbed her hands together like a kid anticipating Christmas. "This is going to be so much fun."

That's not exactly how he would categorize it. This had trouble written all over it.

5

"I AM NEVER GOING TO live this humiliation down," Daisy Mitchell wailed from the depths of the over-stuffed black-and-cream-toile armchair in Martha Anne Sawyer's family room.

Martha Anne didn't know what to say to her best friend. People would talk for some time to come. She simply patted Daisy's shoulder, made a soothing noise and passed a tissue.

Sonya, the wedding planner, had sent Daisy home with Martha Anne. It wasn't the first jilted-at-the-altar situation Sonya had handled and she'd stayed behind to work with the caterer and explain to the guests. According to Sonya it was best if the parents of the bride and groom were kept separated at this point. Martha Anne agreed. She'd always thought Blanton's father was a pompous ass and Beverly Pritchard didn't acknowledge anyone outside her circle of Junior League and Garden Club cronies. Neither one would have been gracious to Daisy.

"I don't know what Andi was thinking," Daisy went on. "Blanton will never marry her now." Yeah, she could pretty much take *that* to the bank, no pun intended. "In fact, no one is going to want to marry her now because they'll all be afraid she'll do the same thing to them." Martha Anne caught her lower lip between her teeth and worried it. She couldn't dispute that either. "She's ruined her prospects. And as if it wasn't bad enough Lola spotted her leaving with Colton in his car. What was *he* thinking? Do you think they planned this, Martha Anne?"

· Martha Anne might not be pleased with her first-born child—well, there was no might to it, she flat out wasn't happy with Colton—but she didn't care for Daisy's tone or implication. "It was a real stroke of bad luck that Lola was the one to spot them." It'd be all over Savannah by nightfall. "But I can assure you it wasn't planned. I don't think Colton and Andi have had any contact with one another for years."

"Well, why'd he have to do something stupid like drive away with her?"

Martha Anne mentally counted to ten. She and Daisy had both been young brides when they'd moved in next to one another more years ago than she cared to remember. Martha Anne had grown up as an army brat who'd spent her whole childhood moving from base to base and she'd learned early on to make friends. Daisy had never been anywhere outside of Savannah. Savannah was her world and she liked it that way. However, they'd discovered they each had a passion for history and homemaking and had become close, fast friends. Both women had said the other was the sister they'd never had. Over the years they'd had their arguments but their friendship ran deep.

Nonetheless, Martha Anne wouldn't tolerate anyone unfairly maligning her child, even if her child was thirty-two, when Andi had clearly been the one to ditch the wedding.

"Daisy, I'm going to give you some leeway because I understand your circumstances, but this is not Colton's fault. He didn't drag Andi out of that window."

Daisy passed her hand over her face. "I know. I'm just distraught."

Martha Anne settled on the love seat opposite her best friend. "He's probably just calming her down and he'll have her back here in no time. You know how responsible my son is." Colton had always done them proud.

"I know. I'm sorry. And if she'd been driving herself she might've wrecked, so if she had to run away, I suppose it's best he's with her. I don't know how I'm even going to talk to that girl when she gets here I'm so upset with her."

Martha Anne suspected Daisy hadn't eaten since breakfast. She pushed up from the love seat and headed toward the kitchen. "I'm going to make us a little plate of cheese and crackers and pour each of us a glass of wine to take the edge off."

The wine would either relax Daisy or put her to sleep, and either way it would be an improvement.

"How about a gin and tonic instead?"

"That would definitely take the edge off," Martha Anne said as she rounded up the cheese and crackers. "But we're going to stick with the wine."

"I've got a lot of edge that needs taking off." Daisy stood and followed Martha Anne into the kitchen. "I called Rion in Afghanistan—"

"Good grief, it would've been around midnight there."

"It was. You know what he said? He said he was glad because Andi needed more of a man than Blanton and then he said he was glad Andi had finally grown a backbone. Can you believe it?" She put her face in her hands and shook her head. "Where did I go wrong? What's happened to my children? I've always been a good mother."

They moved back into the den and Martha Anne placed the cheese and crackers on the coffee table. "Have some," she instructed. "You need to eat," she said as she returned to the kitchen for two glasses and a bottle of previously opened Chablis in the fridge.

Daisy sank back into the chair she'd vacated earlier and munched on the snack. "These are good. What kind of cheese is it?"

"Havarti with horseradish."

"It's got a little kick. I like it." Daisy already sounded better, more normal. Food was the ultimate Southern panacea.

"Eat as much as you want. I have more." She poured each of them a glass of wine and sat back down on the love seat.

Daisy kicked off her pink satin pumps, which had been custom-dyed to match her mother-of-the-bride ensemble. "I swear, I'm just in shock. Shock, I tell you."

"Did you have any inkling this might happen?" Martha Anne sipped at the cool, pale wine.

"No. Andi did come to me with some pre-wedding jitters. She wasn't sure how she felt about him. I told her it'd be fine. Every bride goes through that." Daisy's *sip* polished off half of her glass. "What's not to love? He's from a good family, he has a good job, a nice house and they'd have beautiful children together." Daisy dropped her head to the back of the overstuffed armchair. "And now she's totally ruined her prospects."

Martha Anne slipped off her own shoes and propped her stockinged feet on the coffee table.

"Daisy, you know if Andi decides she doesn't want to get married, it's not the end of the world. It's different now than when we were her age. No marriage is better than a bad marriage." That's why Mattie had moved back in. Her marriage and subsequent divorce had nearly bankrupted Martha Anne's daughter.

"But Blanton—"

Martha Anne had held her tongue far too long. It was time to speak her mind. "Is boring as dirt."

Daisy's head whipped around. "What?"

Martha Anne sipped her drink. "You heard me. He's boring. Gerald was weird with all of his astronomy stuff." Daisy wouldn't be offended by that assessment of her deceased husband, even Gerald had known he was weird. "But he was never boring, for God's sake. Allen was predictable." Had her husband really been gone five years now? There wasn't a day that she didn't miss that man. "You could set your clock by him, but by George he was interesting. Spending time with Blanton is like watching paint dry."

She plopped her feet down and leaned forward to top off her glass and refill Daisy's. "He probably thought I had early dementia last year at that Labor Day picnic because he nearly put me to sleep when I was talking to him." And if a conversation with him was that boring she certainly didn't want to think about what it must've been like between the sheets. "Andi told me once he irons his boxers."

"You're making that up, Martha Anne, just to prove he's a stodge."

"May God strike me dead with a lightning bolt as I sit here. Your daughter told me he irons his underwear…and uses spray-on starch."

"Sweet mercy."

Martha Anne nodded. "Seriously."

"She still didn't have to climb out of a window."

Andi had joie de vivre about her but she wasn't capricious. She had a responsible streak a mile wide so she must've truly felt cornered to walk out on her wedding. Actually, Martha Anne thought she knew where Andi was coming from, as the young set liked to say. "What was she going to do? Come in front of all of those people and have a rational discussion? I don't think she was left with a whole lot of choice, Daisy."

Daisy stubbornly tightened her lips into a thin line of disapproval. "She should've just married him. They would've worked it out."

That was why she climbed out the window. She'd tried to talk to Daisy, and Daisy simply wasn't hearing her. And she certainly wouldn't have heard her at the wedding. "Did you love Gerald when you married him?"

"Yes, I did. You're right. He was weird and I'm not, and we didn't go together but he was unlike anyone I'd ever met before." An indulgent yet sad smile bloomed on her face and the pain of losing Allen stirred once again deep inside Martha Anne. She'd loved like that once…and lost…but at least she'd loved.

"Then how can you possibly expect your daughter to marry a man she doesn't love? That's asking too much."

ANDI ADDED ANOTHER measure of syrup to her pecan waffle but put her fork down. She was full and far too excited to eat any more. She'd denied how she felt about Colton the past several years but there was no denying how alive and on fire she felt now because she was going to have him, and she fully intended to *have* him, all to herself for the next several days... and nights.

"This is going to be fun," she said to him. That blinding moment of actualization at the window when she realized she loved him, that she'd never really gotten over him, had clarified so much about her life and her decisions. "I'm more excited at the prospect of going on a Grand Adventure with you than I ever was at the notion of honeymooning at Sea Island with Blanton." She felt almost guilty for saying it, but she would've felt guiltier still had she gone through with marrying Blanton. He deserved better than a woman who was hung up on another man. And Andi was most definitely hung up on the handsome soldier sitting across the booth from her.

"Then I'd say not marrying him was definitely a good choice," he said with a smile.

"So," she said, pushing her plate to the side. "Where should we go?"

Colton shook his head. "This is *your* great adventure. You decide."

"If you signed on it's your great adventure, as well."

"Look, honey…I mean, Andi." Her heart skipped a beat when that initial term of endearment rolled off his tongue. "I'm just damn glad to be somewhere other than Afghanistan, and after today, it'll be nice to be somewhere other than Mom's for a couple of days. You mentioned Jekyll Island. If that's where you want to go, we'll head that way." He didn't sound particularly sold on the idea. "The last time we were there was the summer before your dad died. Do you remember that trip?"

She did. Colton and Rion had been fifteen and she'd been nine. Mattie, Colton's sister, had taken along a friend. Andi had been the odd man out and she'd been something of a pain in the butt. She definitely didn't want to go anywhere that had those kind of memories. She didn't want him thinking of her as Rion's younger sister with braces. No, she might've blurted it out earlier when Rochelle had asked about a honeymoon but it wouldn't do.

She did, however, have a place she'd always wanted to go that was within reasonable driving distance, and romantic to boot. "What about Gatlinburg, Tennessee? Have you ever been?"

"Never have but I always thought it sounded interesting tucked up at the edge of the Smoky Mountains." He smiled at her across the table and her heart felt as if it flip-flopped in her chest.

Tonight she'd be sharing a room with Colton Sawyer. The very idea made her tingle.

COLTON SLID HIS WALLET back into his pocket after settling the bill, dead-ass certain he was making one hell of a mistake. He was equally dead-ass certain he simply didn't have the willpower to give up the opportunity to spend time with a woman he wanted more than his next breath.

Andi stood at his elbow and it was as if every nerve in his body was tuned in to her—her scent, the cadence of her breath, the healthy glow of her skin, the sparkle in her eyes. Longing rippled through him. No doubt, going with her was foolish, but walking away from the opportunity was impossible.

Colton finished settling the bill and Rochelle rounded the counter. "I just want to wish you both the best of luck. Y'all sure have brightened my day. Heck, I'm gonna give you a hug." The waitress enveloped both of them in a group embrace. "I think you're going to love Gatlinburg. Look, honey," she said to Andi, "you just relax and have a good time before he has to go back to Afghanistan." She winked at Colton. "And you get in a little R & R. Trust me, all the rest of it will work itself out. This ole gal has got a whole lot of living behind her and the one thing I've figured out that's true—don't sweat the small stuff…and it's all small stuff."

Rochelle insisted on treating them as a couple, even though they weren't, but Colton figured that was definitely the small stuff so he let it slide.

Andi offered Rochelle a sunny smile. His

Andi—*whoa, dangerous thinking there, correction*—Andi was a charmer. "It was so nice to meet you. How far is it to the nearest Walmart or Target?"

Rochelle eyed her sympathetically, "I guess you're about ready to get out of that getup, huh?"

Andi nodded. "I can't wait to change."

Colton really, really wished he hadn't heard that. Immediately it brought to mind the image of her standing next to a bed clad only in bra, panties and hose. The idea was enough to damn near break him out in a sweat. Thinking of Andi undressing and/or undressed was someplace he didn't need to go.

According to Rochelle, they were within ten miles of a store where they could do one-stop shopping. After another round of goodbyes and well-wishes they were on their way.

Neither of them spoke as he headed north on the expressway. He pulled out his cell phone. "I'm going to call my mother and tell her not to expect us back today. Much longer and both yours and mine are going to be worried."

Andi drew a deep breath. "No. I'll call. I'm the one who ran. I'm the one who wants to go on this trip. I couldn't talk to her earlier, but now I have to. You can talk to your mother if you want to afterward but I need to make the initial call."

Colton nodded, placing his phone in the middle console. He admired and respected her for that. Andi looked at him. "But I'm going to tell you right now that I have no intention of telling Mom where we're going. She doesn't exactly respect boundaries. She'd be showing up before we could blink. Unfortunately, that means you can't tell your mother either because my mother would hound it out of her sooner or later."

"I'm fine with not telling my mother where I am. I'm a big boy and I don't need to report to her, I just didn't want them worried when we didn't show up." And no, he sure as hell didn't want them showing up.

"Nope. I'll take care of that." Andi turned on her phone. "Wow. Lots of messages. That's no surprise." She scrolled down and pressed a button. "Hi, Mom... Yes, I'm fine. Look, I'm really sorry...You do? You understand? Are you okay...? You think it was unfair of you to expect me to marry Blanton when he's like watching paint dry? Where are you, Mom...? Can you put her on the phone?" Andi said to him, "She's putting your mother on the phone...Yes, ma'am, I am... He knows you're not happy. Is my mother okay? Ah, Chablis. While I have you on the phone, Colton and I are, uh, going to take a detour. We figure we could both use a break so we're going to take advantage of the next few days and take a little bit of time before we head back to Savannah. If you'll put my mother back on the phone, I'll let her know." She held up her right hand, her middle finger crossed over her index finger. "No, ma'am, we're not really sure where we're

going. We're just going to give the dust time to settle
there and drive until something strikes our fancy. Yes,
ma'am, I'll let her know if you hand her the phone
back…Mom? I was just telling Ms. Martha Anne that
Colton and I are going to take a couple of days before
we come back to Savannah…No, we did not plan
this." Another round of crossed fingers. "No, not yet.
No, I'm not going to tell you when we decide…For
goodness sake, Mother, it's Colton."

Thank you, Andi. He'd just been thoroughly emas-
culated by her disdain. As if she'd read his thoughts
she gave him a saucy smile and wink that said she
was simply shutting down Daisy's objections.

"Yes, once we get somewhere and I have some
privacy I'm going to call him…I'm very much aware
I owe him an explanation. Yes, I'm going to call…
No, I'm not going to tell you where I wind up staying.
Mom, I'm going to get off the phone now. I love you…
and you might want to lay off the wine…Yes, I know
you were upset. Yes, I know you had good cause, I'm
just saying. I love you, Mom…I will…I'll call. Later.
'Bye."

She clicked off the phone and looked at Colton.
"Oh, my God. Our mothers must be sucking down
wine like it's water. Your mother was fine but I swear
mine was one step away from being three sheets to
the wind."

"Stress and adrenaline coupled with alcohol will

do that. Obviously they both wanted to know where we're going."

"Of course. So, do you have some girlfriend waiting up in Natick that you need to call to let her know you'll be traveling?"

"Are you trying to find out if I have a girlfriend?"

She dipped her head in acknowledgment. "As a matter of fact, I am."

"I don't. When you know you're going into a war zone for at least a year, it seems unfair to get involved with anyone just to leave them."

"Oh. I never thought of it that way. You know, Colton, some women would consider it an honor to wait on you."

Her words, softly spoken, hung between them, almost as a declaration. He watched the road, but he could feel her looking at him. Emotion thickened the air between them. They passed the exit that would've taken them back home. It felt like passing the point of no return. God knows, his longing for her had reached an all-new level.

"Is that why you've never married?" There was a quiet intensity to her question.

He couldn't lie to her. "In part."

"In part?"

"That and the right woman never was available."

"So does that mean you found the right woman?"

Andi could be as relentless as their mothers. "It

means that's why I'm not married. Don't read more into it than that."

She cocked her head to one side. "You know I had the worst kind of crush on you from about ten to thirteen before you and Rion went away to college."

She'd had a crush on him? "Really?" He'd had no idea.

"You didn't know?"

"No clue."

"Are you serious? I thought you were the best-looking boy in Savannah." She looked at him across the distance of the front seat, her look searing him. He clenched the steering wheel tighter to keep his hands to himself. "I've changed my opinion now."

"That's no surprise." He stole a quick glance at her tempting décolleté. "Considering you've grown up."

"Ah, you *did* notice." The husky note in her voice seemed to stroke along his nerve endings. "I don't think you're the best-looking boy in Savannah anymore." She moistened her lips with the tip of her tongue. "I'd say you qualify as the best-looking man these days."

6

"WHAT DO YOU THINK? Half an hour?" Colton said when they pulled into the parking lot of the supercenter.

He had to be kidding. "At least forty-five minutes. I've got to outfit myself from head to toe—and buy a suitcase." A woman walked by in the parking lot, pushing a cart. She did a double take and then smiled at the two of them. "Not to mention everyone in the store is probably going to stop me because they're going to have a comment or question about me showing up in a wedding dress." A horrifying thought came to her. "I won't be able to try anything on."

"But you know what size you wear." Colton might be logical to the nth degree but he wasn't getting it.

"It's not like men's clothes. Different brands fit differently and sometimes you don't know until you've got something on that it's going to be butt-faced ugly on you or make you look fat." *Think, Andi, think.* She'd always thought well on her feet.

"I don't see how you're going to try anything on with that dress."

She had a stroke of brilliance. "I have an idea and it will ultimately make everything go faster and smoother. You go in and buy me one outfit I can change into. Bring it to the car. We'll drive around to the back of the store and you can step outside while I change in the car. Grab a change of clothes for yourself while you're in there and your shopping will go faster too because I'm sure the uniform gets comments and attention."

"You want me to buy you a dress?"

He was so cute. The man lived in a state of danger and was in command of God knows how many troops, but he looked nearly done in at the prospect of having to buy a dress for her. "Just grab me a dress and a pair of flip-flops. Trust me. This will work so much better than me trailing around in there in this getup."

A family walked by and a little girl with blond ringlets pointed and waved. Her mother and father eyed them with an indulgent smile. Andi automatically waved back.

"I think you're on to something," Colton said. "That dress is definitely an attention grabber." She knew without a doubt the neckline had caught his attention more than once. She'd felt him looking at her. What she wanted, however, was more than looking. With near desperation she wanted to feel his hands and his mouth on her flesh. Likewise she wanted her hands and mouth on him.

"So is the uniform, Major Sawyer."

He gave an exaggerated sigh. "What kind of dress?"

She laughed but there was something sweet and intimate about the moment. It reminded her of some of the exchanges between her own parents that were vague memories. Her parents had been totally devoted to one another.

"Something that fits loose," she said. "I'll write down my dress and shoe size." That was a little embarrassing. She'd tried dieting hard the past month but had wound up feeding her nerves. And, well, eating half the Waffle House menu a while ago hadn't done much to further her diet. "Do you have something I can write on?"

He leaned over to reach past her into the glove box, his arm bumping against her knee, his dark head and broad shoulders temptingly close to her. Her breath caught in her throat and her pulse raced. "Mmm," she said. "You smell good."

Colton closed the glove box and retreated back to his side of the car. "Thanks," he said, his eyes darkening. "So do you." He handed her a notepad and pen, his fingers brushing hers, sending a sizzle through her.

Andi jotted down the sizes and started to pass it back to him. "Wait. Let me make a note on dress colors. No red, orange or gray. I look ghastly in all of those."

"I can't imagine you'd look bad in anything."

Every look, every word made her heart beat faster. "Thank you. I'd rather not prove you wrong on that so let's just skip those colors."

"I tell you what. I'll find a dress, take a picture with my camera phone and send it and you text me back."

Andi grinned. "Got to love that engineering brain of yours. Here's my cell number." She waited until he had his phone in hand and then she gave him the number.

He smiled at her, her coconspirator. "I'll send a photo, ASAP."

She watched him stride across the parking lot, head up, shoulders back, carriage erect. Good grief, but he was beautiful—both inside and out. It was a small wonder she hadn't gotten over him.

And she wasn't the only one who noticed how fine he was. The uniform was an attention getter but so was the man wearing it. Women of all ages in the parking lot turned for a second and third look. That didn't particularly sit well with Andi, not that she had any right to feel territorial, but… And charmingly, Colton seemed totally oblivious. But then again, he was a man on a mission.

Getting out of her dress was going to be another feat that required his assistance. The idea of his hands moving down her back, methodically unbuttoning her dress, exposing her back, sent a rush of heat through her.

Her cell phone rang with a text and she looked at the picture of the dress that appeared on-screen. It was a sunny yellow with cap sleeves, a low-cut bodice that was fitted through the top and then flared out and down. It would look good on her and she was glad he had picked out the yellow. It was a happy color. She texted back Perfect.

Andi knew it would take him a few minutes to pick up his stuff and her flip-flops. She needed to suck it up and call Blanton now, while Colton was gone, and get that off of her plate.

Before she weenied out and changed her mind, she scrolled through and pushed the call button when she got to his name. She thought it was about to go to voice mail when he picked up.

"Yes?" He sounded pissed. Not that she blamed him and not that she had expected otherwise. She'd be equally unhappy if he'd jilted her—well, maybe.

"Blanton, I'm sorry—"

"Do you have any idea how embarrassing that was? I was standing there like a fool when Lola came in and announced you'd just left with Colton Sawyer. Did the two of you plan this? Have you been involved with him?"

"I know it must have been terribly embarrassing and I'm sorry I handled it the way I did. I just didn't

know what else to do because you and I don't need
to be married."

"You picked a hell of a time to reach that conclusion," he said. "That's not true, Andi." His voice
cracked. "Come back, honey, and we'll work this out.
I don't understand. We went through counseling." His
minister had required it. "And we were good. Rever-
end Williams said we were good to go. I thought we
were okay. What happened, honey?"

She'd never felt so torn in her life. It would be so
much easier if Blanton was a jerk, but he wasn't, he
was a decent guy and they'd planned a life together.
How could she tell him Colton Sawyer was what happened? How could she tell him she didn't love him?
How could she tell him she'd thought she was over
Colton but had discovered at the eleventh hour she
wasn't? She wanted some neat, tidy way to handle
this and there wasn't any.

"Blanton, you're a good guy but I realized today I
don't love you the way I should to marry you."

"I think you do. I think you just got cold feet. We
can work through this, Andi."

She wanted to cry. "We can't, Blanton. It's not cold
feet."

"It's Sawyer, isn't it?"

How could she say yes? And of course, the answer
was yes. A thousand fold. And she wasn't about to tell
Blanton that. "No. It's not Colton." And technically
she was wrapped up in Colton but she hadn't been

involved. "How could I have been involved with him when he's been in Afghanistan?"

It hadn't occurred to her that everyone would assume she and Colton were an item when they left together like that. And now that they were going to spend a few days together, tongues would really be wagging. Let them. As men went, Colton was the cream of the crop.

"It doesn't matter. At this point I believe I've dodged a bullet. You're obviously mentally ill."

What? "Mentally ill? You've got to be kidding. Just because I don't want to marry you? That in no way, shape, form or fashion means I'm mentally ill." Dealing with his anger was so much easier than dealing with his pleading. "In fact, based on *that* dumb-ass comment I think it shows incredibly sane, good judgment on my part."

"You're a head case. And by the way, I'm still going on the honeymoon and you can still pay your half of it."

"I don't think so." She'd paid attention to the cancellation policy when they'd booked it. They'd forfeit a couple of hundred bucks for late cancellation but the rest was totally refundable. "I'll pay the cancel fee but you're on your own for the rest."

"Patrice is going with me," he said, obviously expecting the news to wound her. Oddly, the only emotion Andi felt at the news was a bit of satisfaction that her instinct that her maid of honor had a thing for

Blanton had been correct. And this was a far cry from him asking her to come back and work things out. What would have happened to his backup plan with Patrice if Andi had been willing to come back? She didn't care enough to even ask. Patrice was welcome to him.

"Y'all have fun. Tell her she'd better pack some No-Doz."

"Oh, I definitely dodged a bullet. The humiliation was worth not being stuck with you."

Colton was walking through the parking lot. Plus, she had nothing left to say to her former fiancé. "Goodbye, Blanton."

"By the way, my mother wants the string of pearls she gave you back, and I, of course, expect my ring back. And another thing—"

Andi hit the off button, ending the call as Colton opened the rear door. "Your mother again?"

"Blanton. He said I'm obviously mentally ill for leaving him at the altar."

Colton laughed, long and hard. "That's good. You're nuts if you don't want to marry him, right?"

She grinned. "Apparently." She had forgotten how much she loved Colton's laugh. She'd always enjoyed hearing it. It was a rich sound that seemed to come from deep inside him.

"Okay, nut job, let's drive around to the back so we can change clothes."

It couldn't happen soon enough in her book. The

bodice of the dress had been a tight fit to begin with and now that she'd eaten she could hardly breathe. And there was the not-so-inconsequential matter of her needing to go to the bathroom after two glasses of sweet tea.

"I'm more than ready for you to get me out of this dress," she said.

He did a double take. "What?"

"The buttons. I can't unbutton this thing." She reached behind her to her neck and undid the first one. "Well, I can do a couple at the top, and the last half dozen but otherwise I'd have to be a contortionist. Don't sweat it, Major, I'm sure you can unbutton a dress just fine."

HE HAD DEFINITELY NOT signed on for this. Buying clothes for her had been one thing but now he was supposed to unbutton her wedding dress? It was too much. Too intimate. Obviously she had no idea how he felt about her. She had no idea it had been more than a year since he'd actually touched a woman, much less her. And there wasn't a damn thing he could do except sit here and free her from her wedding dress. There was no logical, reasonable way to refuse.

"Can you shift a little more to your left?" he asked.

She canted a little farther in that direction. "Better?"

No, it wasn't better. Andi had undone the top

several pearl closures. Tendrils of her red hair curled against the exposed, pale skin of her neck. The air in the car suddenly seemed thick and heavy with her scent, her mere presence and the desire thrumming through him. He should simply tell her he was taking her home, that he didn't need to be part of her Grand Adventure but he couldn't, he wouldn't.

Instead, mustering every ounce of self-control he possessed, he reached forward and worked the small pearl though the loop. One down, about fifty gazillion to go. He swallowed hard. He could do this. He was a major in the United States Army. She was one woman who needed her dress unbuttoned. He began to mentally recite the army soldier's creed as he moved to the next. *I am an American Soldier. I am a Warrior and a member of a team.*

She had beautiful skin. He refocused. *I serve the people of the United States and live the Army Values.* Distracted, he was careless and his knuckles skimmed her pale flesh. He could've sworn he felt a tremor pass through her, or perhaps that was his own reaction, but there was no mistaking her indrawn breath.

The silence between them vibrated tension. He had the most crazy, irrational urge to test his lips against that soft satin skin he'd just exposed. "So," he said, but his voice came out hoarse and rusty. He cleared his throat and tried again. "So." Much better. "How's work been?"

"It's been good." She sounded breathless. "Actually,

better than good," she continued in a rush. "My online business has exploded and I picked up a couple of new boutiques that are selling on consignment."

Her art. Her jewelry. Earrings and necklaces. "That's…uh…great." Her bra, or at least the portion he'd just revealed, was a white-lace affair with no snaps in the back which meant a man would have to reach between her breasts to unfasten it. *I will always place the mission first. I will never accept defeat.* "So, are you still working part-time at the…uh…other place?"

"I'd quit. I was busy getting ready for the wedding and then Blanton didn't want me working there after we were married, said it didn't look good for a junior executive's wife to work at the mall." She twisted, looking at him over her shoulder. "That was another red flag. Would you do that? Insist your wife not work or be specific about what she could or couldn't do career-wise?"

He paused and her lips parted, a light of inquiry in her eyes, and for the life of him not only could he not momentarily remember the question, he wasn't even sure if he could recite his name, rank and serial number, which was right up there with breathing for a soldier. Oh, right…controlling a wife's career…. "I would never insist she not work or put restrictions on her career, but for a lot of army wives, it's difficult— the moves to different bases every couple of years, the long absences from home. Inevitably whether it's fair or not, the soldier's career takes precedence, and if you're raising a family with one partner gone, that can make a career pretty difficult. So, my career comes with enough built-in limiters for a spouse. I would never throw any out there on my own."

"Some woman's going to be pretty lucky one day when she snags you, Major."

The curve of her back, the indentation of her spine was exquisite. "I'm taking that with a huge grain of salt since you just walked out on a groom you're not currently happy with. I'm sure you thought the same thing about Blanton at one point in time."

She shook her head, sending another curl to rest against her neck. "No, the truth of the matter is that everyone kept telling me how lucky I was, but I don't think I ever felt that way—I'd just been told I was supposed to."

"You think you can manage the rest?" Colton said.

Andi reached around behind her. "If you can get one or two more then I can."

He'd never made such quick work of anything. "Done," he said. She shifted as he spoke, sending his fingers into intimate proximity with her bare skin.

"Thanks. I've got it from here."

He'd never be so thankful to get out of a car. Hastily, his hand not nearly as steady as he'd like, he put the sunshade up across the windshield. "That'll give you some privacy and then I'll stand outside looking the other way and I'll stop anyone who starts to approach the car." He glanced out the window. "Although we're in good shape now. There's no one back here." They were back in the south forty of the parking lot behind the store.

"I'll knock on the window when I'm done and then it's your turn."

He nodded and got out. He was about to slam the door when she said, "I owe you one, Colton. Just let me know if there's anything you need help getting out of."

He closed the door. The only thing he needed help getting out of was this mess he'd gotten himself into with Andi when he agreed to go with her.

7

"WELL, I JUST SPENT a small fortune," Andi said as they met back at the car. It was funny how that worked when you walked out of a place with just the clothes, or in her case wedding dress, on your back. She'd had to grab makeup, toiletries, underwear, a couple of outfits, shoes, sleepwear and a small suitcase. But it had really been kind of fun. It did feel as if she was embarking on an adventure.

"You can always get your money back and we can just head home," Colton said, popping the lid of the trunk open.

"You're out of luck, buddy. You're not getting rid of me that easily," she said with a smile.

He tossed his stuff into the trunk. "And what makes you think I want to get rid of you?"

"Well, we both know you're here under duress." Andi was teasing, but only kind of sort of. She realized she wanted, actually *needed* to hear him say he wanted to be here with her. She laid her suitcase in the trunk and unzipped it.

"Maybe you don't know as much as you think you do," he said, holding the handle of her cart while she transferred her purchases.

She took the bags out of the buggy, putting them in the open case. She'd de-tag and organize when they got to wherever they wound up staying tonight. And she'd be wearing the sexy little nightie she'd purchased just for the occasion. Andi glanced over her shoulder at him, anticipation dampening her between the thighs with a warm, wet heat. "So, you're saying you're excited to be going on the Grand Adventure with me?"

A hint of a smile played about his lips. "Maybe I am."

"You need to learn to contain your enthusiasm, Major," she said, teasing him. It was at least a start and she could feel the sexual energy between them. "It's overwhelming."

Colton pushed the buggy to the cart return while Andi zipped her suitcase and closed the trunk. When he returned he said, "Logistically, I'm thinking we'll just drive tonight until we decide to stop and then finish the trip tomorrow."

She nodded. They didn't have any set agenda, simply a destination in mind. That's what made it an adventure. And the main thing was being with him. "That works for me. And I can drive for a while. I actually like to drive. I find it relaxing. I prefer driving to sitting in the passenger seat."

"I'm more than happy to turn the wheel over to you." Colton handed her the keys and rounded the car to the passenger side. He paused, glancing at the rear seat. "Do we need to keep your wedding dress hanging in the back?"

"I'm not really comfortable with putting it in the trunk," Andi said, getting in the driver's seat. He got in as well, closing the door. They both buckled up. "It's going to need to be cleaned because I was sweating like a pig but trunks can be pretty dirty and I'd rather not get any kind of stain on it that might be questionable coming out." She started the car and headed back toward the interstate, bringing them that much closer to their first night together. "Not that the trunk looked particularly dirty or anything, but the dress is white and that can be a stain magnet, if you know what I mean."

"I hear you. It's fine in the back." He'd neatly folded his dress uniform and it lay on the backseat next to her dress. He'd picked up a pair of jeans and a collared knit shirt in a mocha color that looked great with his tan and his green eyes. She'd meant to tell him so earlier. She fully believed men liked compliments just as much as women did. "By the way, I like that shirt on you. It looks good with your tan and your eyes."

"Thanks," he said. "It's nice to wear something other than army-issue for a change. That yellow looks good on you with your hair." The look in his eyes more than echoed his words.

"That's sweet of you to say." She glanced at herself in the rearview mirror. "This updo's a little formal for the dress but I don't dare try to take it down until I've got a shower at my disposal." She laughed. "I'm not even sure it would come down. I believe she used about a gallon of hair spray to shellac it in place. I could probably go through a wind tunnel and it wouldn't move."

Colton laughed. "It looked good for your big day… well, your almost big day. So what happens now?"

"What happens now what?"

"Your future. Your plans changed just a little bit this afternoon. You said you'd moved back home until the wedding but you're obviously not moving in with Blanton now."

"Ah, you mean the logistics of an aborted wedding." Andi shook her head. She'd never even entertained what happened when you ditched at the last minute. "I have no clue. I guess the presents go back and I've got some decisions to make as to where I'm going to live. I can assure you, I'll be moving back out right away. Ms. Daisy's not going to be a happy camper."

"I thought you said she was kind of okay when you talked to her earlier."

"That was because she'd had some wine. Once it wears off she'll be unhinged again. That's part of my plan on my big adventure, to decide what I'm going to do next. Sometimes stepping away from a situation for a couple of days is the best way to handle that." She didn't say it to Colton but she felt as if she was at an important juncture. Going back to what she'd had before, what she'd been, suddenly seemed as impossible as marrying Blanton.

"What will you do with the dress?" Colton was so practical. That was the kind of thing he'd think of. "My mother had her wedding dress altered for Mattie even though she thought Mattie was making a big mistake, which it turned out she was. Are you going to hold on to it for another time?"

Andi laughed. "Heck no, I'm not holding on to it. It's got bad juju for me now." She'd figured this out earlier when they were in the store. "I'll sell it online. And since I've already embarrassed myself and the whole family, I'll probably list that it never actually made it through the ceremony. It'll go like a hotcake. I'll probably get close to what I paid for it since it comes with a story."

Colton shook his head laughing. "Not to stereotype but sometimes you women aren't the most rational creatures."

"It's just a different rationale," Andi said. She didn't expect him to understand because it was a totally different way of thinking than he employed. "You wanna find a radio station? I'm good with pretty much anything except classical music, heavy metal and hard-core rap."

Colton reached over and turned on the radio with a smile. "No problem because I can't say that I'm a fan of any of that either." He scanned through a couple until he found a country station. "You like this?"

"Yep. The lyrics tell a story. Well, I guess with most songs the lyrics tell a story but I usually prefer the stories they tell in country music."

"Well, it's always nice to be able to understand them." She could feel him looking at her. "So, back to your story, you said you couldn't marry Blanton because you didn't love him and he was boring. Did you figure that out by comparison?"

He'd lost her. "By comparison? Do you mean like seeing my girlfriends in relationships?"

"Is there someone else you're interested in? Some-one you realized you're in love with and that's why you couldn't follow through with marrying Blanton?"

She could see his logic, his reasoning, and she could feel the heat of a blush climbing her neck and face. She should've known he was far too rational not to reach that conclusion. She hedged because she wasn't ready to tell him how she felt about him—quite frankly she didn't know whether what she felt would be substantiated by her time with him or whether it would prove antidotal. The next couple of days with Colton would either sink her or free her, and he most certainly didn't need to know that. "I think it's plenty that I figured out I didn't love him, and if I don't love him, I shouldn't marry him. Isn't that logical?"

She looked away from the road just long enough to glance at him. "Absolutely logical," he said, his expression inscrutable.

"I'm glad I'm not here with anyone else," she said. "I'm glad it's you."

"Why?"

"Do you realize you and I have never spent time alone together?"

"Maybe that's a good thing."

"No, I don't think it's a good thing at all. I think this is all working out swimmingly." She hesitated for a moment, the full impact of what he'd said hitting her. "Why would it be a good thing you and I were never alone together?"

"What purpose would it have served?"

"Does everything have to serve a purpose?"

"Pretty much, yes."

That didn't just sting, it hurt. She knew she was skating close to the edge. She hadn't slept well in weeks. She'd been majorly stressed managing the wedding and her mother. She'd run the emotional gamut of realizing she loved Colton, running away from her own wedding to finally having some time with him only to have him make some thoughtless remark. She knew she was past herself, past her coping limit, but she didn't quite know what to do about it. "So, you don't think there's any merit in getting to know me better? I think you're about to hurt my feelings up one side and down the other." She forced a laugh. She would not cry. Granted she was emotional because it had been an emotional day. She'd made a huge decision about her future, pissed off a ton of people, rediscovered the feelings she had for the man next to her were very real and very intense. She'd thought she'd detected an equal attraction on his part, but apparently she was mistaken. Apparently she was forever destined to be the little sister and she knew with blinding clarity that's what she'd been dancing around with Colton all afternoon.

She wanted the man he'd become to see the woman she'd become. She wanted it in the worst way. She wanted *him* in the worst way. And he'd just told her point blank he wasn't interested in getting to know her better. Nope, she wouldn't cry…at least not now… but it stung like the dickens. "Actually, I think you just did hurt my feelings up one side and down the other."

He rubbed his hand over his cropped hair. "Dammit, Andi, I didn't mean to."

"It's okay. I know you didn't." Crap. Her voice was thick with unshed tears.

"Are you crying?"

"No. I am not crying." Close, but no cigar. She put on her blinker and moved into the right lane. There was an exit in one mile. She'd get off there.

"Andi—"

"Just do us both a favor and don't say anything else, Colton."

Mercifully, the mile passed quickly and the radio helped fill the terse silence stretching between the two of them. She slowed and took the exit ramp.

"What are you doing?" he said.

"You know you have the most annoying habit of questioning the obvious." It was easy to let anger fill the space created by hurt. "I'm climbing out of a window at my wedding and you want to know what I'm doing. I'm getting off on an exit ramp and you want to know what I'm doing."

"Okay, *why* are we getting off of the exit ramp?"

"Because I'm taking you back to Savannah." She wanted him and she wanted this time with him but not under these circumstances. She thought they'd reached a different agreement and apparently she'd been wrong.

"Don't you mean us?"

"No. You. I'm going to go by Blanton's house and get my car. He and Patrice should be gone by now—"

"Can you just pull over for a minute?"

She pulled the sedan into a gas station and put the car in Park. "Happy?"

"As a lark. Now, who the hell is Patrice and where are she and Blanton going?"

"Patrice is…was my maid of honor. They're going

to Sea Island, which is where he and I were going for our honeymoon."

"And now Patrice is going with him? How do you feel about that?"

He'd just stomped on her heart and he wanted to know how she felt about Blanton going to Sea Island with Patrice? She wanted to shake him. "I'm fine with it. I'd thought for some time Patrice had a thing for him. So, they should've already taken off for Sea Island and even if they haven't, they can't stop me from getting my car. Once I have my car, you can go wherever you please, with whomever you please and I will be on my merry way, alone."

"And what happened to me going with you?"

"No thanks."

"And you changed your mind why?"

"You said you didn't want to get to know me better, which leaves one other possibility. Colton who always does the right thing is going to babysit the runaway bride on his leave because it's the right thing to do." She was so disappointed and frustrated she could scream. She'd dared to hope, to think that he was interested, that there was something between them.

"You don't know what you're talking about, Andi."

"Of course I don't. I'm just little Andi Mitchell and—"

He closed the space between them, his hand cupping her head. "Does this feel like I'm doing the right thing?" he said seconds before his mouth claimed hers in a startlingly honest, hungry kiss. Long before she was ready for him to, he tore his mouth from hers. "See, Andi, I don't always do the right thing."

Her lips tingled and her heart soared with renewed hope. Fireworks—it had been like the sparkling finale.

She curved her hand around the nape of his neck and leaned in until her lips were nearly grazing his, until his warm breath mingled intoxicatingly with her own. Unchecked hunger glimmered in his eyes and pulsed between them. "That's where you're wrong, Major, because nothing has ever felt more right."

She took up the kiss where he'd ended it.

HE'D DONE WHAT HE'D SWORN he'd never do. Colton had crossed the line with Andi. Unfortunately, he now knew without a shadow of a doubt just how incredible her kiss could be. She tasted like a spicy-sweet forbidden fruit. Her answering hunger and passion, the way her lips felt beneath his—those would forever be imprinted in his memory bank, in his senses. Reluctantly, he ended their kiss again.

He couldn't help himself from brushing his fingers over the fine smooth skin of her cheek before dropping his hand back to his lap. Kissing her had been reckless and careless on his part. He wouldn't, however, make the same mistake twice. Well, actually he already had. But he wouldn't repeat his lunacy a third time.

"We're not going there again, Andi," he said, mentally arming himself to withstand what he knew was sure to be an argument now.

"Okay," she said.

There was nothing wrong with his hearing, but perhaps he'd heard her incorrectly. "Okay?"

"Sure. We won't go there again." She looked altogether too smug, and his Andi, the woman he knew, would've never capitulated so quickly. "I told you I was crushing on you when I was younger. I always wondered what it would be like to kiss you. Apparently, you always wondered what it would be like to kiss me, too. So, now we both know." She shrugged as if to say *no big deal*.

That was good. Great, in fact, but she'd said nothing had ever felt that right. "But you said—"

"I know. It did feel right. It could've been a little longer, but overall it was a heck of a kiss. But if you don't want to kiss me again, it's okay. I'm not going to beg any man to kiss me, regardless of how good it was. Not even you."

Damn her, she was twisting his words. "I didn't say I didn't *want* to kiss you again."

"Colton, you said we weren't going there again."

"But that doesn't mean I don't want to."

"I'm so confused. If you want to and I want to—

and I'm not making any bones about it, I'd sure like to—why wouldn't we?"

He didn't think for a minute she was confused but she sure as hell had him all tangled up. She was talking circles around him.

"You know good and well why not."

"No, I don't. For a man of logic and reason, you're not making a bit of sense."

"You're off-limits. You've always been off-limits." Dammit, that wasn't what he'd meant to say. "I'm too old for you. Our mothers are best friends and your brother is my best friend."

She shook her head, obviously not buying into it. "I'll be the first to admit when I was twelve, you were a little long in the tooth for me. Even when I was sixteen and you were twenty-two, that would've been a huge gap but come on, give me a break. I'm twenty-six and you're thirty-two. That's perfectly acceptable." She glanced around the car. "And I don't see either of our mothers or my brother here. Besides, I know Rion made out with Mattie at least once because I saw them."

Rion and Mattie? What the hell? And was Colton totally clueless when it came to what was going on around him? Apparently so. "When was this?"

Andi waved her hand in dismissal. "Oh, roughly sixteen years ago or so. And now what? Does that make you want to go find him and protect her honor or something? Does that change anything between the two of you?"

He was surprised, but that was it. "No." But that was in part because they'd made out as teenagers. They hadn't been involved in anything more. Rion was his best friend but Colton wouldn't appreciate his friend applying his same love-'em-and-leave-'em standards to Mattie that he did to the other women in his life.

"Seriously? Knowing that didn't ruin your friendship?" She feigned shock. "You haven't lost all respect for him? I don't know what to think."

"Very funny." And even though he was the object of her mockery, it *was* funny. Andi had always had a good sense of humor. And he wanted to make sure she knew exactly what their situation was. "You realize you're rebounding?"

She shrugged off his comment. "If that's what you want to think. I consider it celebrating my good sense not to marry a man I don't love and then to kiss a man I've been wanting to kiss for years."

Although her words were light and playful, he could feel her longing, so like his own, that had been held at bay for years. "You're killing me, Andi."

"That's not my intent, Colton. Now, you tell me what it's going to be. Do I take you home or do you go with me? If I thought I'd get away with it, I'd kidnap you but that's not going to really work out well and I don't want you under those conditions." Her smile never failed to tangle him up inside. She bridged the gap between them and placed her hand on top of his. Her touch echoed through him. "I don't want you coming with me because I've forced you or because you feel obligated to look out for me. If you come with me I want it to be because you want to spend time with me, because you want to get to know me. So, what's it going to be? I'll respect whatever decision you make with no hard feelings."

There wouldn't be any hard feelings but there'd sure as hell be hurt feelings. But where would they both be at the end of this trip? The bottom line was he desperately wanted this time with her. And when would they ever have this opportunity again?

He could spend time with her without crossing that line again. It would be a chance to get to know the woman she'd become before he returned to Afghanistan. They could be friends. He turned his hand so they were palm to palm and clasped her hand in his. "I want to go with you."

"You're sure? You're not just being nice?"

"I'm sure and there's nothing nice about it." Her smile was like being handed a prize. "Now are you going to put this car back on the road, because you can't have a road trip without doing that, or do I need to drive?"

8

"I DON'T LIKE IT. I don't like it one bit. At all," Daisy said, shaking her head, perched on a bar stool in the kitchen. "What do they mean they're going to take a couple of days before they come back home?"

Martha Anne, browning ground beef and garlic at the stove for spaghetti sauce, loved her best friend, but the woman could be very trying sometimes. "Well, I think they mean just that. You were fine with it earlier."

"But now that I've had a nap and sobered up, I've changed my mind," Daisy said, sipping at a glass of iced tea.

Daisy had slept for over an hour. "Honest to Pete, Daisy, they're both adults." Martha Anne pulled tomato paste and canned tomatoes out of the pantry. She'd been a little taken aback by the news when she'd talked to Andi, but Colton had always been like one more big brother to Andi. "And I can't say I much blame either one of them for not wanting to rush back so you can tear a strip of hide off of them. And I'll include myself there, as well. Colton was probably just as happy to give me time to chill, as Mattie likes to put it."

"Well, that's part of the problem. They are both adults. It's a matter of decorum. How's it going to look to everyone that they're off together?"

Everyone in their circle of friends and acquaintances knew how responsible Colton was. Heck, it would probably only enhance Andi's reputation that she was with Martha Anne's son. "Daisy, need I remind you that Andi's near-miss—that would be Blanton—has taken off for their honeymoon destination with the maid of honor in tow?" Lola, the town crier, had called earlier to break the news. "Who in the heck is going to really care that Andi isn't here for a couple of days?"

Mattie came in through the kitchen door from the garage. "What's up?" She washed and dried her hands at the kitchen sink.

"Your mother has lost her mind, that's what's up," Daisy said, crossing her arms over her chest. Martha Anne opened the cans while Mattie grabbed a glass from the cabinet. "She doesn't seem to find it a problem that my daughter and your brother have decided to take a few travel days together before they come back home."

Mattie paused in the middle of putting ice in her

Get 2 Books FREE!

Harlequin® Books,
publisher of women's fiction,
presents

HARLEQUIN® Blaze®

GET 2 BOOKS

We'd like to send you two *Harlequin® Blaze®* novels absolutely free.
Accepting them puts you under no obligation to purchase any more books

HOW TO GET YOUR
2 FREE BOOKS AND 2 FREE GIFTS

1. Return the reply card today, and we'll send you two *Harlequin Blaze* novels, absolutely free! We'll even pay the postage!

2. Accepting free books places you under no obligation to buy anything, ever. Whatever you decide, the free books and gifts are yours to keep, free!

3. We hope that after receiving your free books you'll want to remain a subscriber, but the choice is yours—to continue or cancel, any time at all!

EXTRA BONUS

You'll also get two free mystery gifts! (worth about $10)

FREE!

Return this card today to get
2 FREE BOOKS and 2 FREE GIFTS!

 HARLEQUIN® *Blaze*

YES! Please send me 2 FREE *Harlequin*® *Blaze*® novels, and 2 free mystery gifts as well. I understand I am under no obligation to purchase anything, as explained on the back of this insert.

About how many NEW paperback fiction books have you purchased in the past 3 months?

❏ 0-2
E9RD

❏ 3-6
E9RP

❏ 7 or more
E9RZ

151/351 HDL

FIRST NAME	LAST NAME

ADDRESS

APT.#   CITY

STATE/PROV.   ZIP/POSTAL CODE

Visit us at:
www.ReaderService.com

(H-B-03/11)

If offer card is missing, write to: The Reader Service, P.O. Box 1867, Buffalo, NY 14240-1867 or visit www.ReaderService.com

BUSINESS REPLY MAIL

FIRST-CLASS MAIL   PERMIT NO. 717   BUFFALO, NY

POSTAGE WILL BE PAID BY ADDRESSEE

THE READER SERVICE
PO BOX 1867
BUFFALO NY 14240-9952

NO POSTAGE
NECESSARY
IF MAILED
IN THE
UNITED STATES

glass, glancing from Daisy to Martha Anne. "You're kidding, right?" she said.

Pursing her lips, Daisy said, "I wish I was."

Mattie's eyebrows shot up. "Well, that is news. Not as big as the news about Blanton and Patrice, but still…." She poured tea into her glass from the pitcher sitting on the kitchen island.

Martha Anne gave her daughter a sharp look. "I'm sure your brother is just looking out for Andi."

Mattie sent them an incredulous look. "You both do know that Andi's had a crush on him for forever?"

"My Andi?" Daisy said. "No. You're off the mark, Mattie."

It was news to Martha Anne.

Mattie propped against the doorjamb. "You'll need to double-check that, Ms. Daisy. Remember when I used to babysit her? She kept a diary."

"Dear God, you read the child's diary?" Daisy said.

Humph. Martha Anne barely bit back a snort. Daisy would've read it in a heartbeat if she'd found it.

"Of course," Mattie said, matter-of-factly. Sometimes Mattie reminded her so much of herself. "But it wasn't as if I went looking for it. She left it open in the den one night after she went to bed. She'd only written *Andi loves Colton* about a million times and had drawn all the squiggly hearts and stuff."

"That was a long time ago," Daisy said with a sniff.

Mattie nodded. "It was and Colton's definitely uglied up since he was eighteen."

"Sarcasm is totally uncalled for, young lady," Daisy said.

"Well, she does have a point." Martha Anne added the canned tomatoes to the skillet. "Colton is an attractive man." He looked so much like his father. "And if she had a crush on him once upon a time..."

"My Andi's a beautiful woman."

"There's no disputing that," Martha Anne agreed. Andi had definitely grown into her own. There had been a time when the child was awkward but she'd matured into a vivacious woman with her dark red hair and lovely skin so like Daisy's. Martha Anne added the tomato paste and a generous amount of oregano and basil.

"I'm fairly certain Colton's noticed," Mattie drawled. She looked from one mother to the other. "Am I the only one who noticed the way the two of them were looking at one another the last time he was home and Andi was around? It was right before he was shipping out to Iraq that first time." She sighed and shook her head at the expressions on their faces. "Apparently I was. Okay, consider this. Andi had six gorgeous available attendants today and she and Blanton have a slew of friends. But Colton insisted on driving separate. He told me he was cutting out right after the ceremony to go to Ray-Ray's. Why doesn't a guy who's been stuck in camp Afghanistan for a year not want to be at a party afterward with lots of attractive twentysomething females? Give me a break. We all saw *Wedding Crashers*. A wedding reception is the easiest place in the world for a single guy to pick up a date."

Martha Anne had never entertained the thought. "You think Colton and Andi—"

"No," Daisy interrupted. "Absolutely not."

Although Daisy was overreacting, she had had a trying day. Much as Martha Anne hadn't wanted Mattie to marry Marcus, it would've still been awkward and embarrassing to have had her climb out of a window and leave them all waiting and then to have to explain to several hundred guests that there wasn't going to be a wedding that day. So, she understood Daisy's nerves were shot, but still...

"Maybe Mattie does know something we don't, Daisy." Martha Anne smiled. "They'd certainly make a nice-looking couple and Andi would keep Colton on his toes and that's just what he needs." She'd been waiting for years for her son to find the right woman. If that woman was Andi, Martha Anne couldn't be more pleased.

Daisy's composure seemed to dissolve right before them. "I'm sure you're wrong. You have to be wrong."

"Now, wait a minute, Daisy. Exactly what would be so terrible about Andi and Colton getting together?" They were both adults. Andi was a nice girl and Colton certainly beat Blanton Pritchard hands down in the man department.

"What would be so terrible? It would be a disaster."

Really bad day or not, Martha Anne didn't care to have a relationship with her son defined as a disaster. "Mind yourself, Daisy. Colton is my son and I don't see a thing about him that lends itself to disaster."

Daisy stood, her back uncompromisingly rigid. "Colton's already taken one of my children halfway around the world. I'll be hanged if he's taking Andi, too."

Martha Anne reduced the heat on the stove to low and turned to face her friend across the kitchen island. They were going to get this thing straight right now. "You've inferred before that Colton's the reason Rion went into the military. My son didn't talk yours into anything. And joining the army is probably the best thing that could've happened to Rion, so you may want to rethink your position, Daisy."

"He's too old for Andi."

Perhaps at one time, but not anymore, as she'd just deduced a minute ago. "That's ridiculous."

"What? You want them to get together?"

"Just because they're taking a little trip together does not mean they're going to get together—"

"Yes, it does," Mattie threw in.

Martha Anne merely glared at her daughter for

stirring the proverbial pot and continued. "But my son is a fine man and a damn-good catch."

"He's wrong for Andi."

"Well, you didn't exactly hit a home run when you picked out Blanton, now did you? Because we all know he was your choice."

"I still say he would've made her a fine husband. He has a good job—"

"He's a *junior* bank executive." Martha Anne stood ramrod straight. "My son is a *major* in the United States Army."

"And he's from a good family," Daisy finished on a spiteful note.

"I'd rather be a DeWitt—" Martha Anne's side of the family "—or a Sawyer any day than a Pritchard. You are skating on thin ice, Daisy Mitchell."

"I'm going to find my daughter and bring her home."

"That's it," said Martha Anne, "you've truly lost your mind. Andi is twenty-six, not a sixteen-year-old runaway." Lord, this had shades of when Rion decided to join the military. "Give her some breathing room, Daisy."

"I will not have her getting involved with Colton. I simply won't have it. That would mean her moving and I want my children near me, not scattered to the four corners of the world. I'll find her and bring her home. I believe Andi's phone has GPS. Can you help me with that, Mattie, dear?" Daisy said.

Martha Anne didn't give her daughter an opportunity to respond. "Matilda Eugenia Sawyer, you will not help this crazy woman track down her poor beleaguered daughter."

Daisy bristled. "Did you just call me crazy?"

"Well, your mind may be gone but there's certainly nothing wrong with your hearing."

"It is not crazy that I don't want my daughter involved with your son."

Enough. She wouldn't stand here and have her son impugned in her home, best friend or not. "Daisy, it's time for you to leave. You are no longer welcome in my home."

Daisy slammed the door on her way out. Mattie stood wide-eyed. "Mom, wow, I didn't think... Is she going to have another freak-out the way she did when Rion left?"

An eerie sense of déjà vu washed over Martha Anne. "I don't know, Mattie. I don't think so. I hope not."

"Mom, I think she needs help. Do you know how much pressure she put on Andi when Rion left?" Mattie shifted from one foot to the other. "When I used to babysit Andi she'd talk all the time about how she was going to travel and see the world. Half the time I'd tune her out because I was sixteen and way more interested in my world, but I do remember that."

Martha Anne stood stock-still, considering Mattie's words. Sometimes you were so close to a situation or a person, that you couldn't clearly see the changes going on in front of you. Sort of like seeing someone every day and not noticing they were losing weight until you didn't see them for a period of time and then it smacked you in the face when you did see them.

Daisy had spent months barely leaving her bed after Gerald's death, and Martha Anne and Allen had done all they could for her and gladly taken care of Rion and Andi. But they'd given her space to recover on her own. She'd similarly taken to her bed when Rion had left, although not for as long. Once again, Martha Anne had given her time to mourn and recover. But now, through Mattie's words and eyes, Martha Anne saw that perhaps Daisy hadn't truly recovered.

Perhaps Daisy did need professional help, but cooler heads and a good night's sleep were needed before that subject was broached. And if Mattie was correct and Andi and Colton were attracted to one another, all hell was bound to break loose.

EXHAUSTION TUGGED AT ANDI. Although the early-spring sun had already sunk below the horizon, it was still fairly early evening. "Let's look for a place to stay for the night. My day is really catching up with me," Andi said from the passenger seat. Colton had taken over the driving when they'd stopped to fill up the gas tank. "I need a shower and a bed." And you.

Ever since that kiss, she hadn't been able to think of much else. And she knew it was on his mind, too.

She felt it in the way his gaze lingered on her mouth, in the flicker of desire he couldn't seem to control in his green eyes. The air between them seemed to fairly hum with want and need…and denial.

"Are you hungry?" Colton said.

Only for you—for another kiss, for your touch, for the warmth of your skin against mine. "No. I'm still full from earlier. What about you?"

"Same here." And she could swear he was echoing the same hunger for her. "So, what kind of accommodations do you require for the evening?"

"My big requirement is clean. We're just going to be there one night."

"Clean works for me, too. Pickings may be sort of slim because we're about fifty miles from the next sizable city."

"I don't have another fifty miles in me right now." They passed a billboard advertising The Daisy Inn at the next exit. Andi nodded. "Why don't we check that out? It sounds kind of picturesque." And there was an irony in that it was her mother's name.

They pulled off of the interstate and looked at one another at the stop sign at the top of the exit ramp. The Daisy Inn sat within spitting distance of the interstate, across the street from the Roadside Truck Stop. "We might as well check it out. We'll look at the room and if it's not satisfactory then we'll just keep driving," Colton said.

"Do you have a flashlight in the car?"

Colton made the left and looked at her questioningly. "In the glove box, if the batteries aren't dead. Why do we need a flashlight?"

"Bedbugs." Andi couldn't suppress a shudder. "Haven't you read about them?"

"It hasn't been an issue where I've been," Colton said on a dry note.

"Yeah. I guess you've been worried about slightly bigger issues—like staying alive."

"There's always that."

Now that they were here, she was slightly nervous. Who was she kidding? She was about to check into a motel with a man she'd wanted forever, and who seemed to want her to some degree. She was a crazy mixture of apprehension, excitement and near exhaustion.

Colton drove beneath the covered pull-through in front of the office door. The place looked as if it had been originally built in the sixties. "I'll go in with you," Andi said. She was more than ready to stretch her legs. They climbed out of the car and the sound of music floated across the air. In an adjacent empty lot, a group of teenagers sat on the tailgates of several pickups, country music playing on a radio turned up loud enough for all of them to hear it. All of the boys sported ball caps except for one who wore an oversize cowboy hat.

"Guess it's something to do on a Saturday night, huh?" Colton said.

"I suppose," Andi said, even though that had never been part of her teenage experience.

Colton held the door for her and they both went into the brightly lit office. A bouquet of fresh daisies sat in a green vase on the countertop. It was a nice touch. Andi thought it portended good things to come. A dish of potpourri accounted for the scent of apples and cinnamon. A quilt of daisies, which looked handmade to Andi, who recognized an original art piece when she saw it, hung on the wall.

An older man, Andi would put him in his late sixties or early seventies, sat behind the desk watching Brit-com reruns on a television set. The man was thin with a fringe of gray hair around his head. He stood, a welcoming smile revealing a perfect denture smile. "Howdy. Welcome to The Daisy Inn. I'm Burt Pickle, owner and proprietor. Me and the wife, Vernette, are glad you folks stopped in." He gestured toward the daisy quilt. "Vernette does all the quilts in the inn and even sells a few now and then. I'll tell ya, them big chains have about run us out of business, but we're still hanging in there." He paused momentarily for breath, sizing Colton up, but the pause wasn't long enough for Colton or Andi to speak up. "You a military man? You look like a military man. I can spot 'em." Mr. Pickle stood a little taller. "I'm a veteran myself. Korea." He pronounced it Ko-rea. "And Vietnam. Yessir, seen plenty of action. You been to Iraq?"

"Yes, sir," Colton said. "Two tours in Iraq and I'm in Afghanistan now."

"Vernette," Mr. Pickle bellowed, nearly causing Andi to jump out of her skin—she was already on edge. "Come out here. We got us a bona fide war hero here." He lowered his voice. "She's started losing her hearing but she's still the finest-looking gal in Ritchie County."

Vernette, her gray hair in a braided coronet on top of her head, came in from a door in the center of the room. Vernette stood as wide as she was tall. But the light in Burt's eyes when he looked at her said he did, in fact, see the finest-looking gal in Ritchie County. Andi must've been tired and emotionally overwrought because she thought it was incredibly sweet and romantic and it almost made her cry.

"Welcome, welcome, welcome," Vernette Pickle greeted them. "It's so good to have company."

She made it sound as if they were long-lost friends who'd dropped by for dinner.

"This here's a war hero home on leave from Afghani-stan," Burt said loudly to his wife.

"Well, my goodness," Vernette said, looking at the two of them. "How long are you home for?"

"I have to report back for duty on Friday."

Andi knew it but hearing it spoken aloud made her feel faintly sick. Colton was here for such a brief period of time.

"Guess you're mighty glad to see him, aren't you, hon?" Vernette said to Andi.

Andi looked at him and didn't bother to mask the feelings in her eyes. "Yes. I am. I'm mighty glad to see him."

Even with the Pickles there, his eyes held an answering glimmer.

Vernette beamed at them. "Every one of our four children was born nine months after Burt was home on leave. He's a rascal. I bet yours is, too," she said to Andi. She looked at her husband. "Set these fine folks up in the honeymoon suite." Andi held her breath, waiting for Colton to protest or tell the Pickles they needed two rooms, but he didn't speak up and the moment passed when Vernette continued. "By golly, I know what it's like to have your man home for a short time." She winked at Andi and adopted a confiding tone. "It's the only room with a king-size bed and mirrors on the ceiling."

"It sounds perfect," Andi said somewhat desperately, as in desperately hoping he didn't protest. She didn't dare look at Colton. Her, him, one big bed and mirrors on the ceiling—the idea set her on fire.

"I think you'll find it so. I clean every room myself once a week, whether it needs it or not. Kinda getting hard with the arthritis in my knees but you won't find a cleaner room anywhere. And we don't have bedbugs." Andi must've looked surprised. "Oh, I know it's an issue. Me and Burt are on the internet and we stay informed. I know some folks do but I check regularly." Vernette nodded with satisfaction over the room's state of cleanliness.

"That's good to know," Andi said.

Vernette smiled, patting Andi on the hand. She turned to her husband. "Come on, Burt, let's show 'em to their room."

Colton held up his hand, "You don't have to do that. There's no need for you to get out after dark."

Burt Pickle shook his head. "Oh, yessir, we do. That's the way it should be done. That's what sets us apart from the others." Burt pulled a key off the hook with a room-number tag hanging off of it. No keyless entry at The Daisy Inn.

Burt and Vernette insisted on walking out with them. "Son, you want to pull the car down? It's the room down on the far end," Burt said, pointing a bony finger in the direction where the teenagers were congregated in the empty lot next door.

Vernette winked again. "That way you don't have to worry about whether you're too noisy or not."

Andi just smiled weakly. She could feel her face flushing at this woman commenting on she and Colton having noisy sex and…well, at the thought of having noisy sex with him.

Colton opened the car door and the interior light illuminated Andi's wedding dress in the backseat along with his folded uniform.

Vernette didn't miss a thing. She lit up like a

Christmas tree. "Burt, would you look at that? This here couple is newlyweds. Y'all shoulda told us. Good thing we're putting you in the honeymoon suite. Burt'll bring you down a bottle of champagne and a honeymoon basket."

Andi opened her mouth to go through the convoluted story of slipping out of her own wedding and then deciding to take a trip, but Burt cut her off before she could get a word out.

"Vernette keeps one cold in the fridge—a bottle of champagne, that is. She drinks it once a month."

"That's on account of wanting to keep it fresh. You can't expect champagne to keep much past a month. And if you share it—" She shot Burt a look. "Well, it keeps the marriage fresh too, if you get my drift. We haven't had any honeymooners come through, in a blue moon. How long's it been since we had honeymooners, Burt?" She looked back to Andi, shaking her head. "My memory's not what it used to be."

Burt smiled indulgently, apparently unperturbed by his wife's lack of memory. "About two years. I think that's when Vonda Kay and Randy Simmons tied the knot." Burt glared at the collection of pickup trucks in the lot next door, down on the end of the honeymoon suite. "Ding-dang kids got nuthin' better to do than loaf around," he grumbled.

By the time they made it down the sidewalk that ran in front of the motel doors, Colton stood waiting, having parked the car in front of the room and taken their suitcases out of the trunk.

Burt opened the door, stepping in and flipping on the light. He held the door for them to enter. Vernette brought up the rear.

"Wow," Andi said, looking around. "This is pretty…wow."

Vernette preened. "I've added on over the years until I got it as romantic as possible."

It was an eclectic mix of brothel, antiques and country charm. Red bulbs, definitely a brothel touch, glowed from the bedside lamps flanking the bed, which was covered in a king-size wedding-ring quilt. Sure enough, a number of twelve-by-twelve-inch mirrors had been mounted above the bed. A basket of silk daisies sat in the middle of the table for two tucked in the corner. Gingham panel curtains with daisy trim hung at the windows.

Andi immediately had a good feeling about the room. And the artist in her was drawn to the quilt. She stepped closer and examined it. It was craftsmanship work, the stitches perfect, the pieces sewn flawlessly, the colors all melding. "This is beautiful," she said to Vernette.

Vernette blushed. "Well, thank you. It's just a little hobby and I figured I might as well put them to good use."

She dropped Andi a wink and turned to her husband. "Come on now, Burt. Let's skedaddle and give them some time alone." She paused at the door. "Burt'll be right back with your champagne and honeymoon basket."

The Pickles stepped out, closing the door behind them, and Andi forgot all about the quilt. Tension and anticipation swirled around them, between them. It was just her and Colton and one very big bed...with mirrors on the ceiling.

9

IT SUDDENLY FELT INCREDIBLY hot in the room with the door closed. Andi was still standing by the bed but Colton was very much aware that Burt would be returning soon to deliver the basket. Colton turned on the air conditioner. "Let's get some air circulating in here."

It was stuffy with everything closed. Hell, maybe he was warmer than normal, perhaps because he'd lost sight of normal somewhere along the way. His normal was burying his feelings for Andi, keeping the attraction at bay, not acting on it. His normal was remembering she was his best friend's sister, that he was a soldier who'd be going back into a war situation, that she'd always been off-limits, that they didn't have a future together.

And somehow, somewhere along the line all of that had shifted. Was it when he'd helped her run away from her wedding? Was it the moment he decided to come with her? Was it unbuttoning her dress or those two potent kisses? Or the yearning that had swirled and wrapped around the two of them all afternoon until he'd wondered if he had lost his last bit of rational thought?

All he knew was he could've and should've told Burt Pickle they wanted two rooms. And he hadn't. And how the hell was he ever going to share a bed with Andi and keep his hands off of her? The bottom line—he wasn't keeping his hands off of her any more than she was staying away from him. They didn't have a future but they had now...and the next five days.

Slowly, deliberately he crossed the room and Andi stood still, waiting on him. In the back of his mind flitted the thought that she'd been waiting on him a long time, the same as he'd been waiting for her. And now, the waiting was over.

Colton reached out and cupped her cheek and jaw in his hand. She felt like warm flannel beneath his palm. She closed her eyes, as if she was savoring his touch, then turned and pressed a kiss into his hand. It was as if something snapped in each of them simultaneously, as if a dam broke.

Andi was in his arms, her lush curves molded against him. He kissed her, his mouth devouring hers, his kisses greedy, hungry. Andi strained against him as if she shared his gnawing want.

They fell back onto the bed together and he rolled so he was on the bottom and absorbed her weight.

For a moment it was as if everything slowed and then stilled to that moment with the press of her body against him, her scent surrounding him, the taste of her mouth against his tongue, the sound of her breathing meshing with his. Her heart beat against his own, the two beats melding into one.

Andi looked at him. Her brown eyes flecked with green seemed to peer into his very soul.

Colton reached up to bury his fingers in the richness of her red hair…and his fingers got stuck.

"Ouch," she said.

He yanked his hand back. "Sorry." That's right, she'd had it professionally done for the wedding.

For a second Andi looked embarrassed, then she laughed. "Go figure," she said. "I've waited a lifetime for this moment and I've got so much goo in my hair, your hand got stuck." She rolled off of him to the edge of the bed. "We've waited this long, another few minutes won't kill either one of us. I'm going to hop in the shower." She stood, her knit dress clinging to the curves of her hips and ass, her nipples outlined against the soft material hugging her breasts.

"You've got to undress anyway. Take your dress off here," he said hoarsely.

Andi shook her head, a siren's smile curving her lips and lighting her eyes. "No. If I take my dress off here and now, we both know I won't make it to that shower, and I need to. I'll be right back. Hold that thought," she said with a pointed glance at his crotch, where his erection was making its presence known.

Colton watched the play of fabric over her body as she crossed the room and grabbed her suitcase.

"Trust me. This thought will still be right here," he said.

Her smile promised very, very good things to come in the near future. "I won't be long," she said as she closed the door.

It didn't escape his notice that while she'd closed the door, he hadn't heard the lock click.

Just on the other side of the door, she was skimming that yellow dress up her hips, along that same expanse of her sweetly indented back he'd revealed earlier when he'd unbuttoned her. The sound of running water came from the bathroom, followed shortly by the noise of the shower.

He sat up on the edge of the bed. Maybe she needed a little help in the shower with those hard-to-reach places. He rolled to his feet, fully intending to join her in the shower when a knock sounded on the door and Burt called out, "Room service."

With the muted noise of the shower in the background, Colton crossed the room and opened the door. Burt handed him a basket and plastic ice bucket full of ice. "This is what Vernette calls the honeymoon package. The champagne's cold but you'll want to keep it chilled after you open it."

"Thanks so much," Colton said. At first glance he

saw a champagne bottle, two plastic glasses...and handcuffs trimmed in hot-pink fur.

Apparently Colton wore his surprise on his face because Burt nodded knowingly and clapped him on the shoulder. "Yep, Vernette sure can do some shopping on the internet. Oh, and the champagne is screw cap. Every time we had to pop that cork, it scared the bejesus out of Vernette so we finally went to the screw cap."

In the other room, the water stopped. Even though Colton appreciated the gift, Burt needed to leave now. Colton hoisted the basket in acknowledgment. "Thank you."

Burt clapped him on the back with a smile. "Just ring the front desk if you need anything."

Colton closed the door behind the other man and slid the locks into place. The air conditioner wasn't quite as loud as a freight train, but it definitely drowned out any hint of noise outside. At least they wouldn't hear interstate traffic all night.

He crossed the room and placed the basket on the table, at a loss as to how to proceed. And he was never at a loss. He didn't want to just jump on her like a starving dog with a juicy bone but that's about how he felt. They could at least start out with a champagne toast...before he jumped on her. He pulled out the bottle and glasses. Vernette had included candles, as well. Candlelight would work, too. Colton made quick work of putting the bigger candles next to the bed and some of the smaller ones on the dresser and the round table. After lighting the candles, he killed the rest of the lights in the room.

The candles flickered and danced in the dark and the ones next to the bed were reflected in the overhead mirrors. He'd unscrewed the champagne and poured each of them a glass when the bathroom door opened and Andi emerged from a cloud of steam. She saw the candles and reached behind her, turning off the bathroom light before she walked farther into the bedroom.

Colton's breath hitched in his throat. She was beautiful. Her hair hung in damp, dark red curls past her shoulders. A short black nightgown and a robe knotted at her waist showed off the shapely length of her legs, her delicate collarbone and the base of her neck and the creamy rise of her breasts.

"You're beautiful," he said as she slowly crossed the room.

"So are you," she said, her voice low and quiet, no trace of teasing there.

He held out a glass of champagne. She took it, her fingers brushing against his. A tremor ran through him. Their gazes tangling, he lifted the champagne glass. For as short-lived as the two of them together would be, he meant for it to be good.

"To us."

ANDI RAISED HER GLASS, touching the plastic to Colton's. She echoed his toast, loving the way it sounded, loving the implication, especially since it was coming from him. "To us."

She sipped. He was about to be hers…finally…at least for the next five days. The champagne was sweet and cool against her tongue. But it wasn't champagne she wanted against her tongue.

Both she and Colton put their glasses on the table and moved into one another's arms of one accord. He was warm, solid masculinity. He sighed, his warm breath stirring her hair and teasing against her temple. Burying his hands in her hair, he scattered kisses over her face and along her jaw. Andi was melting inside. She wrapped her arms around him, her hands seeking and learning the contours and lines of his body.

Their lips met and it was as if they'd tuned into the same station, as if they were coming from the same place. His kiss was tender and reverent, yet hungry.

Andi immersed herself in the feel and taste of his lips. His tongue teased at her mouth and she opened herself to his quest. He swept the moist recesses of her mouth and her entire body responded. The damp heat between her thighs intensified and her breasts felt sensitized.

With a small moan, she rubbed against Colton, loving the feel of his hard chest against her nipples through the material of her gown and robe, the press of his erection against her belly and the top of her mound.

He dragged his mouth from hers and murmured on a ragged breath, "Put your arms around my neck."

As soon as she was holding on, he scooped her up. In three strides he'd closed the distance between the table and bed. Bracing on one knee, he lowered her to the bed, following her down to the mattress. The quilt's surface was cool beneath her heated skin.

She glanced up and caught their reflections in the mirrors on the ceiling above them. At first she'd thought the mirrors over the bed tacky. They now struck her as erotic.

She smoothed her hands over the back of his close-cropped hair and then down his back. She tugged at his shirt. "I want your shirt off," she said.

He levered up to sitting position. "Your wish is my command," he said with a slightly wicked grin. Grasping the shirt at the bottom, he pulled it over his head in one fell swoop.

With a dual sense of wonderment, she reached her hand up and smoothed it over his chest. It was amazing that after all these years of pent-up longing and fantasizing and masturbating herself to orgasm thinking of him, she was actually touching his bare chest. Her other sense of wonderment was that his chest was even better than she'd fantasized. He was a lean man but he boasted a muscular upper body. Not only was his chest a delicious mix of satin skin stretched taunt over lean muscle, but he had just the right amount of hair sprinkled over his chest and then down his tight, flat abdomen. She tangled her fingers in his chest hair and said precisely what was on her mind. "You are one incredibly sexy man."

"I'm glad you think so, but, honey, you're the one. You take my breath away." Reaching between them, he tugged on the end of the belt she'd knotted about her waist. Her robe fell open. In the flickering light, his eyes glittered as he looked down at her. His action deliberate, he used one finger to slide the narrow strap of her nightie and the edge of her robe over and down her shoulder. The touch of just one fingertip against her skin and she was wound even tighter inside.

She lifted just far enough off of the mattress to slip out of the robe. She settled back on the quilt. "You were saying…"

The sound he made was something between a sigh and a moan as he lowered his head to kiss the edge of her shoulder. A shudder rippled through her at the sensation and warmth of his mouth against her nakedness.

Her breath quickened and her pulse raced as he worked his way down to the rise of her breast. His lips were warm against her skin. Andi closed her eyes and arched her back, desperate for him. Rather than slide the material farther down, he captured her nipple in his mouth. She sucked in a steadying breath as he enveloped her turgid point in his warm, wet mouth, the sensation arrowing straight from her breasts to her thighs.

Colton repeated the same on the other side. Andi had never known her breasts to be so sensitive. At one point she nearly came as Colton licked and sucked her nipples. She fisted her hands in the quilt, crying out.

He stood and divested himself of his shoes and socks. Andi, her body humming with want and need, knelt on the mattress and pulled back the covers on the big bed. The sheets were a soft white cotton.

Her nipples tightened even more, the room's cool air teasing against the wet material of her gown where his mouth had been. Still kneeling, Andi turned her attention to Colton. He was just stepping out of his jeans, revealing trim hips and leanly muscled, well-shaped thighs and legs. The rigid line of his penis stood outlined against his dark BVDs.

She wet her lips with the tip of her tongue, nearly quivering with the need to touch him, to have him once again touch her. The hum of the air conditioner formed a backdrop of sound. Colton, looking at her, hooked his fingers in the band of his briefs, tugged them down and stepped out of them.

His penis, thick and long, saluted her from a thatch of dark hair. His scrotum hung full and heavy beneath. She swallowed a moment of trepidation. He was considerably larger than what she'd left behind at the altar and her one other experience before that. One thing was for sure: Major Colton Sawyer wasn't a card-carrying member of the Little Dick Club.

She didn't stop to think, she simply acted on instinct. She knelt farther on the bed and reached out. She slid one fingertip down the length of his erection. Wrapping her hand around him, she gently tugged him toward her until his knees were almost touching the mattress. She stroked up and back down, loving the feel of his hot cock against her hand and fingers.

This wasn't just any man, this was her man. Keeping her hand on him, she leaned forward and pressed kisses onto his beautifully sculpted chest. She teased her tongue against his male nipples and his cock surged in her hand. Ah, he was as responsive to that as she was. She drew his nipple into her mouth and sucked. Once again his member quivered in her hand and she wrapped her fingers just a little tighter around him and stroked.

She kissed her way down his belly to the outside of his hips, stopping to lick and suck his skin along the journey. With each touch of her mouth and tongue to his body, she felt him tense. Andi paused, inhaling his total masculine scent. She hadn't put on any panties beneath her nightgown when she'd dressed after showering. She was dripping wet between her thighs, awash in need and desire.

All this time, she'd focused on simply his body—his chest, his belly, his hips. Now, she looked up at him. The flickering candlelight darkened his green eyes, but it was *her* that left them glittering with heat.

Deliberately, she looked back down and lowered herself, aching to taste him. She delicately licked at the base of his cock and then swiped her tongue up his rigid length. She was thoroughly turned on by his scent, the velvet heat of his penis against her tongue and the sound of his muffled groan followed by his broken, "Oh…Andi…honey."

He buried his fingers in her hair, cupping her scalp, but not tugging her forward. She was free to take things as far as she wanted to. She caught the drop of moisture with the tip of her tongue. His essence was slightly salty. Steadying him with her hand wrapped lightly around his base, Andi took him in her mouth… or rather as much as she could. She wanted to give him pleasure. She wanted him satiated. She wanted to love him in every way a woman could love her man.

She moved her mouth up and down his erection, setting a rhythm between her hand and mouth. She loved the taste and feel of him in her mouth and moaned her pleasure. Colton's harsh breathing punctuated the air.

And then he stopped her. "Andi…no…not the first time…not this way."

She rose to her knees. She understood. She'd been totally into him and what she was doing, but no, she didn't want their first time to be that way either. She wanted him buried deep inside her. She grasped the hem of her gown in her hands and pulled it up and over her head, tossing it aside.

"Andi," he said on a husky, awe-filled note looking at her fully naked for the first time.

It was the right thing to say. She'd come to terms with the fact she was never going to be one of those model-thin girls and had accepted she was a woman with curves, some in places she didn't particularly care for, namely a muffin-top. Apparently Colton was fine with curves.

"I want to feel every inch of you against me, in me," she said, wrapping her arms around his neck and pressing close to him. She rubbed against him, reveling in the sensation of his hair-roughened chest against her nipples.

His mouth captured hers in a hot, hard, demanding kiss…and she loved it. Lost in the sensation of his mouth and tongue and the hard press of his body, she found herself on her back.

Colton braced on one arm to keep his weight off of her. He stroked and smoothed his other hand over her breasts, down the curve of her hip. He paused as the tips of his fingers brushed the edge of her pubic hair. "Oh, you are wet." He explored farther, lightly running his big finger along her nether lips. She was so ready for him, so aching, she shuddered beneath his touch, arching her hips up to bring his finger into more intimate contact with her body.

"That's what you do to me, Colton Sawyer. That's

the effect you have on me. That's how much I want you."

He positioned himself between her thighs and nudged at her wet channel with the head of his penis. "And this is how much I want you."

"Show me more," she said, widening her legs and canting her hips to meet him, a welcoming committee of one.

He froze. "Protection."

"I'm on birth control and the other should be fine if you're okay."

"I'm good. It's been a long time."

His eyes caught and held hers as he eased inside her. She gasped and he immediately stopped. "Am I hurting you?"

She shook her head. "No, it just feels so good, so right."

"It does, doesn't it?" he said as he pressed the rest of the way home.

It was as if they had been custom-made for one another. With each stroke, with each in and out, Andi felt as if he was loving her, as if he'd never touched or made love to another woman the same way he was with her now. And with each thrust and slide where she met him she was giving him the same thing— herself, as she'd never given herself to another man.

She was growing tighter, tenser, climbing higher and higher with him and she felt herself teetering on the brink when he said, "Come with me, Andi. Cum for me."

He reached between them, found her clit with his finger and stroked it while he moved in and out of her. She felt as if her body went into slow motion as she slowly, exquisitely came undone and unraveled at the same time Colton did.

10

COLTON PULLED Andi closer, his arm beneath her head, his other arm wrapped around her middle. He nuzzled her shoulder and inhaled the fresh scent of her hair. It had been one helluva weird day. He'd started it fully expecting her to marry another man and he'd ended it making love to her. The day had definitely taken a turn for the better.

It had certainly been a heck of a day for Andi, as well. "How are you?" he said.

"I'm wonderful," she said, pressing a tender kiss to his arm. She wiggled her bare backside closer to him and sighed. "Maybe a little tired, well, a lot tired, but wonderful nonetheless because I'm here with you. What about you? Are you okay?"

God but she was sweet and sexy and, for now, his. He tightened his arm about her. "I'm better than okay." Making love to her, being inside her, feeling her hands and her mouth on him—it had been infinitely better than he'd ever even imagined, and he'd imagined plenty. "Although I may get up in a minute and hit the shower." But he wasn't ready to move just yet. For now he wanted to enjoy the experience of lying in bed and holding her in his arms.

"There's nothing quite like a hot shower, is there?"

He traced his thumb over the swell of her breast and smiled into her hair. "Well, there are a few things that are better." She offered a short chuckle at his gentle teasing. "But yeah, showers are pretty damn nice. It wasn't until I did my first tour in Iraq that I realized just how attached I am to a hot shower. Any shower, for that matter."

Andi stroked the back of his forearm with her fingertip. "Rion said the same thing." She gave him a searching look in the mirrors above the bed. "Do you want to talk about being over there?"

He shook his head. "No. Thanks for asking but I don't. I'm not trying to shut you out but when I get to leave it behind for a little bit, that's a good thing. Our work there is important but I want to be one-hundred-percent here with you now." That was another thing he'd learned quickly in a war situation. Living in the good moments when they were there...'cause you just never knew when your time was up.

He'd told her he didn't want to talk about his time in Iraq or Afghanistan, and he didn't. But one of the things he carried with him inside—one of the things aside from ripping Andi's family apart, if they had any kind of future, if she'd have him—was the count-less times he'd seen fellow soldiers with wives and children waiting for them at home lose their lives. At least if a bullet, bomb or IED with his name on it found him, he wasn't leaving behind a wife. He wasn't being critical of the men who were married, it was simply his choice not to do that. He would not ask a woman, namely this woman, to wait for him while he was in a war zone. An old-timer had told him once that if the military wanted a man to have a wife, they'd issue him one. He had to say there was some merit to that. He put aside the thought, deliber-ately bringing himself back to the precious moment at hand.

"Mmm, I'm glad you're a hundred percent here with me now," she said. She offered him a smile in the mirror, her eyes heavy with satisfaction and sleep. "I think I'll take a quick nap while you're in the shower."

"You do that, baby." He pressed another kiss to her shoulder, extricated his arm and tucked the cover around her. "You comfy?"

She nodded, her eyes already closed. "Yes, but it'll be better when you're back in bed with me."

He rolled out of the bed and stood there for a mo-ment, watching her simply because, for now, for the next four days, he had that privilege. Her red hair, a tangle of curls, fanned over the pillow. The alabaster curve of her shoulder peeked out from beneath the quilt. He could happily watch her drift off to sleep every night for the rest of his life. But some things just weren't meant to be.

ANDI STARTLED AWAKE, momentarily disoriented. She looked around. Where was she? Ah. The Daisy Inn in South Carolina. She'd heard something. That's what had awoken her. She heard another sound from the bathroom and realized it was the sound of the running water, of the shower. That must've been what had awoken her.

She checked the bedside clock. Two-fifteen in the morning. She'd maybe been asleep fifteen minutes tops but she felt refreshed and invigorated. She wasn't so sure that it was as much the nap as the man in the other room and the driving need to make as many memories with him and for him as she could in the next few days.

On a whim, she rolled out of bed. They were about to make another memory. She relit the pillar candles on the bedside tables—he must've extinguished them before he'd gone into the shower. That was the kind of thorough, safe man he was.

Working quickly she pulled on the lace-topped thigh highs she'd worn earlier in the day, a white lacey thong, the plunging white front-hook push-up bra and her white satin pumps. Hose and heels made her feel sexy and she had a hunch Colton would like them, as well.

She snagged her brush and dragged it through her hair, bringing some slight semblance of order to it. She clipped it loosely up, a few pieces falling down around her shoulders.

The shower stopped in the bathroom and she hurried over to the bed. Colton didn't strike her as a man to linger after he finished showering. Stretching out on the bed on her side, her heart began to thump against her ribs and moisture gathered between her thighs in anticipation.

The bathroom door opened and he stepped out wearing a pair of underwear. He stopped short when he saw her.

"I was through with my nap, so I thought..." She trailed off.

He grinned and crossed the room in a few short strides. "I definitely like the way you think." He joined her on the bed.

"Mmm...you smell good," she said. She stroked her hand over his shoulder and down his chest, his skin and hair still moist from the shower. "And you feel even better."

He slid behind her, spreading his legs on either side of her, his back against the pillows and headboard.

"Speaking of feeling good..." It seemed the most natural, the most right thing in the world for Colton to stroke and caress her skin until he was cupping her bra-clad breasts in his hands. He smoothed his thumbs over the tops of her breasts that spilled over the edge of her lacy cups. Reaching between, a smile curving his sensual mouth, he released the hook. In seconds her bra joined the rest of their clothes on the floor.

Colton, his breathing hard, wordlessly pulled her in between his legs and turned her so that her back was to him, her buttocks between his thighs. "Lean back on me," he said, cupping her heavy breasts in his hands.

She knew exactly what he was doing…and she liked it. She leaned back and looked up. She'd only thought she was turned on before. His skin was naturally darker than hers and hours spent in the sun had left his arms and hands darker still. They were a marked contrast against her paleness. Her red hair spilled across her shoulders and his chest.

She felt the heavy beat of his heart against her back, heard the uneven cadence of his breathing, which echoed her own. Her eyes caught and held his in their reflected image. Slowly, deliberately he toyed with her nipples until she was arching against his questing fingers.

She was burning for him. "Touch me lower," she said.

He brushed his hands down the plane of her belly to stroke her thighs. She rocked her hips in silent invitation. Fascinated, incredibly aroused, she watched as Colton delved his fingers beneath the edge of her panties. There was something terribly, terribly erotic in watching from the mirror as she experienced the tactile sensations. She gasped aloud when he found her wet, slick channel. His moan resounded in her ear.

"Take them off," he said.

She slipped them off and down her legs, one side tangling on her ankle until she kicked it off. She leaned back against him again and spread her legs, any vestige of modesty long abandoned to passion.

They both watched as his sun-kissed fingers stroked and toyed with her pink glistening flesh. And then his thumb found her clit and the orgasm that had been building and building exploded inside her. As the first tremor shook her, his voice was low and urgent in her ear. "Look at me," he said.

She focused on him, on them as she found her release.

"That was…incredible," she said, when she could finally speak again. "But not fair to you."

"Oh, honey, it was more than fair. Do you know what I felt like watching you come and knowing I was the one that took you there? And it's about to be fairer still, if you're up to it."

"Up to it? Why wouldn't I be?"

"I didn't know if you might be sore. If it doesn't feel good we'll take a break."

Had there ever been a man who was more thoughtful and sexy and just generally wonderful? "I think it will feel just fine."

"Move down a little bit and then turn to face me."

She did as he instructed.

"Slide back toward me and put one of your legs under mine and the other one on top of mine."

Once again, she followed his instructions. She didn't wait on him to tell her to slide forward, she figured out that part all on her own.

She leaned back, bracing on her elbows, watching in the mirror as his penis nudged against her wet curls and orgasm-drenched pussy.

"Oh, honey…" he said, his face tightening. Bit by bit, he entered her, giving her time to adjust, to stretch, and take him all. One thing was for sure, she was wet enough.

She dropped her head back. "Oh, God, you feel good."

"Not nearly as good as you feel."

He shifted his hips and began to move inside her. She'd thought she'd just make him happy and bring him to his release. Amazingly, she felt another orgasm began to build. She wasn't sure who cried out the loudest when they both came.

Andi collapsed on her back. "That was… I've never…ohmigod."

"I read about that once when I was researching, but never tried it."

"Researching what? Sex?"

"Well, yeah. That's how you're informed. You study and research. I thought it sounded interesting—you know, to bring your partner to back-to-back orgasm."

She'd never loved his logical engineering geeky mind more. "Well, I'll be interested in learning more about your research."

THE NEXT MORNING Martha Anne was surprised when she walked into the den and spotted Mattie in the kitchen. It wasn't her daughter's favorite place to be. Even more astonishing, however, was the unmistakable scent of coffee and baking muffins.

"Morning, Mom," Mattie said. "The coffee's ready, blueberry muffins are almost done and I've got the pan ready for poached eggs."

Martha Anne peered over the top of her glasses. "What happened to my daughter and who are you?"

"Very funny, Mom. I know what happened yesterday, about you and Ms. Daisy, was upsetting. So, I guess this is my way of saying I'm sorry. Well, you know, in addition to actually saying I'm sorry because I'm the one that brought up Andi's crush on Colton."

"Apology accepted, even though unnecessary...and I like my eggs medium, white set, yolk runny." It was a nice change to have someone preparing breakfast for her.

Mattie grinned. "I've got it covered."

Martha Anne took out her favorite coffee cup and moved through the ritual of preparing it just the way she liked it—sweet and with lots of half-and-half. Her coffee to her satisfaction, Martha Anne settled on a bar stool while her daughter moved about in the kitchen.

Her back to Martha Anne, Mattie spoke from where she was in the kitchen. "I know you were disappointed when I married Marcus and I know it's embarrassing for you to have me divorced, broke and living back home at my age…" Mattie didn't actually cry but her voice thickened and her eyes teared up on the last bit.

"Honey, I was disappointed when you married Marcus. I wasn't disappointed in you, simply in your choice. I want you to be happy. I want you to have what your father and I had. You deserve a man who appreciates you for the bright, beautiful woman you are, and I knew that wasn't Marcus." She paused to sip. "Good coffee, by the way. Now as to being embarrassed by you living at home. That's definitely not the case. I hate it for you, because I think *you* find it embarrassing but I'd ten times rather have you back home with me than staying with a man who was bankrupting you financially and emotionally just because you thought you had nowhere else to go."

"Are you sure?"

"Honey, you're a paralegal and a fine one at that. I'm proud as punch of you. You know part of it is that Colton reminds me so much of your Daddy while, honey-bunny, you definitely didn't fall far from the tree. Sometimes we're so much alike, you and I, that we lock horns but that doesn't mean I love you any less."

"I just know Colton never got in trouble as a teen-ager...well, wait, let's just qualify that he never got in trouble."

"Well, that's because he's got that logical, reasoning engineer's brain the Sawyer men seem to have. Colton doesn't get into trouble because he's slow to make decisions. He has to consider every angle and every nuance before he takes action. And there's no devilment in the boy, whereas you and I, and I'll throw Andi in there too, we've got far more devilment in us. We're more creative and impulsive and sometimes it gets us in trouble."

"Thanks, Mom," Mattie said, hugging her. "I think we needed to have this talk."

"Oh, if you thought I found you an embarrassment or disappointment, we definitely needed to clear the air."

"Why is Ms. Daisy so crazy?" Mattie transferred the eggs to the waiting plates and added a muffin. "She's serious about not wanting Andi and Colton to get together." She joined her mother at the breakfast bar.

Martha Anne had lain awake in her bed last night thinking about her friend into the wee hours of the morning. "We all know Daisy had a hard, hard time when they lost Gerald. There was no warning. He simply left that morning for a conference and was lost to them a few hours later. Savannah is her world, it represents home and safety. She sees the rest of the world as…well, threatening. She's very insular. It's really just fear, Mattie. She feels if they stick close to home, they'll be safe. She's terrified she's going to lose Rion in this war and so that's just making her clutch Andi even tighter."

Mattie nodded. "I guess I understand a little better now, but doesn't she know she could drive Andi away in the end?"

"I'm hoping Andi walking out on the wedding like that and taking a few days is going to make Daisy realize she's got to give her space and let her make her own choices."

"Colton's interested in her."

Martha Anne shook her head. "You know, there was always such an age difference I never considered it, but when I think back on it he was a little hostile almost when I'd fill him in on the wedding details. And I was surprised he wasn't going to stay for the reception." Mattie's eyes widened. "Oh, yes, I heard him tell you but it was surprising because—"

Mattie rolled her eyes, but it was in good humor, and cut her off to finish the thought. "—because he always does the right thing."

Martha Anne laughed, nodding. "Pretty much. So, maybe he does have a soft spot for her. I don't know."

"He's my brother and I love him and I do know he's a good-looking guy but he's so boring."

"No, honey, you missed that conversation with Ms. Daisy. Blanton is boring—"

"Amen to that."

"Your brother, much like your father, is predictable. He's stable and that's not a bad thing, but they're far from boring. They're men a woman can count on."

Mattie buttered another muffin and passed half of it to Martha Anne. "Well, it wasn't predictable when he took off with Andi, was it?"

"Actually, in a way it was. Andi needed help, and knowing Andi, my guess is she was going to take off on her own if he hadn't gone with her."

"Damn." Mattie looked disgusted her brother hadn't actually behaved impulsively. "You're probably right."

"Watch your mouth and don't look so disappointed. There's still time for him to prove me wrong."

Mattie shook her head. "Andi and Colton, go figure."

"I didn't see it coming," Martha Anne said. She eyed her daughter speculatively. "Now there was a time when I wondered if you and Rion might not have a mutual interest…."

Mattie developed a sudden interest in getting up and putting away the leftover muffins. "Just typical teenage stuff."

"I see."

"No, seriously, Mom, don't use that tone. It was no big deal. He *was* the first boy I ever kissed. I can assure you, however, I wasn't the first girl he kissed."

"I don't doubt that. Rion had girls after him from the time he started kindergarten. He's always been a charmer. That's why I think joining the military was so good for him. It forced him to develop some good habits because charm doesn't get you far in the army."

"Obviously, 'cause no one, not even you, his mother, would ever accuse Colton of being charming, and he's a major."

"I'm going to take that in the vein of good humor."

"That's the way it was meant."

Martha Anne watched her daughter's face closely while she spoke. "It certainly was a shame Rion couldn't make it home for the wedding."

Mattie shrugged. "Things usually work out the way they're supposed to."

"But it would've been nice to see him. It's been almost nine months."

Mattie handed her the leftover blueberry muffins

in a plastic zip-top bag. "Why don't you take these over to Ms. Daisy and y'all kiss and make up."

"I'm not sure I'm ready to do that just yet."

It did not escape her notice, however, that her daughter had steadfastly ignored her comment about Rion.

11

"WHAT TIME DO YOU WANT to leave?" Andi asked Colton, propped on one arm. Her hair tickled against his chest.

He, who was used to the regimentation and schedule of the military, found himself oddly content to just lay in bed with Andi. Actually, the notion of making love again before they left was vastly appealing.

He pulled her on top of him. "I'm not in any hurry to leave this morning." He slid his hands up the backs of her thighs to cup her bare ass in his hands. "How about you?"

She kissed his neck and rocked her hips against his suggestively. "I'm in no hurry at all."

The moment was shattered by a harsh knock on the door.

She licked the base of his throat and murmured, "Just pretend we didn't hear that."

A succession of rapid knocks sounded. "I don't

think we can ignore that." With a sigh he rolled her back off of him and stood, pulling on his jeans and shirt.

Much as he liked Vernette and Burt Pickle, and it had to be one of them, this damn well better be good.

Colton threw the locks and opened the door. Sure enough, Burt stood on the other side, his hand raised, ready to knock yet one more time.

"Oh, good. You folks are up and dressed. I just wanted you to the know, the police are on their way and we've got everything under control." Colton didn't have a clue what Burt Pickle was talking about, but Burt continued without giving Colton a chance to speak. "I can't tell you how sorry I am this has happened," Burt said.

"I don't know what's happened," Colton said.

"Your car, son, your car." Burt moved out of the way and Colton got a good look. It was everything he could do not to laugh. He would've expected this in perhaps the wrong section of any city, but here? Ritchie County, South Carolina? His father's sedan sat in the parking lot…on concrete blocks. The tires had been stolen.

"Well, this is certainly unexpected."

"I know it was those ding-dang kids. But don't you worry, the police are on their way and we'll have these recovered for you in no time. They'll just come take a report and once we've tracked those hooligans down, you can go down to the police station and identify your stolen property and be good to go."

That was precisely how Colton had no intention of spending his day. "Burt, those tires needed to be replaced anyway." Well, they probably had another five thousand miles of tread left but that was about it. "I'll just buy a new set and we won't worry about it." The kids had probably just taken them for a lark and then thrown them in a ditch somewhere.

"Oh, no, sir. This is bad for my establishment's reputation. Word'll get around that you get your tires ripped off when you stay at The Daisy and then who's gonna want to come? Oh, no, sir. We'll get to the bottom of this."

"But I really do need to just put on new tires."

"Well, Maynard Polk has the tire store over in town but he don't open on Sundays and this being Sunday, he's not open. As soon as I file the police report, I could take you to Marchette, it's about a forty-minute drive, and we could pick up some tires for you. We'll come back and put 'em on and then you'll have to drive back to Marchette to have 'em balanced."

To the best of his estimation abilities, considering Ritchie County's finest had yet to show up so Burt could file his report, that would effectively eat up the next four to five hours of the day. In the meantime, there was a perfectly good bed and Andi right here. He'd waited a hell of a long time for her and he wasn't willing to waste that kind of time when their time was already limited.

"Can you give us a minute to discuss this?" he said to Burt.

"Sure thing."

Colton stepped back into the room, closing the door behind him. Andi sat in one of the chairs, dressed. "I heard," she said.

"This is your Grand Adventure so it's your call. I know you wanted to get to Gatlinburg—"

"I'm not nearly as concerned with getting to Gatlinburg as I am with spending time with you. Let's just stay here and wait for Maynard Polk to open in the morning."

Her answer pleased him so much he couldn't help but tease her. "I don't think there's a lot to do here, especially since we don't have transportation."

"I'm so sure we can find something to do to pass the time. After all, you've got your book and I've got my crossword puzzle."

"And don't forget cable."

"Right. We can always watch bad television."

"Hold that thought. I'm going to step out here and see if Burt'll let us stay in the honeymoon suite one more night."

"I'll be waiting."

"I'm counting on it."

Colton stepped back out onto the sidewalk where

Burt stood, his arms crossed over his chest, eyeing Colton's tireless vehicle mournfully.

"Burt, Andi and I talked about it and we'd like to stay over another night, if the room's available. We'll wait on Mr. Polk to open tomorrow. It saves you a heck of a lot of driving and we were very comfortable last night."

"Even if it wasn't available, I'd make it available but heck yeah, y'all are more than welcome to stay tonight and don't worry about tomorrow, we'll do you a late checkout."

"We appreciate it."

"Well, let's just get it straight. Tonight's on the house."

"Absolutely not. You're saving me money because we both know Gatlinburg's going to be more expensive, so staying here tonight actually keeps a little extra in my pocket."

They heard them before they saw them. Lights flashing, sirens wailing, two county police cars pulled into The Daisy's parking lot.

"Howdy, Burt."

Burt nodded, "Clifton." He nodded to the other deputy. "Larry."

"Are you the owner of this car?" Clifton said.

"Please tell me the crime scene hasn't been disturbed," Larry said. "I need to dust for prints, take photographs and some measurements."

Larry bore an uncanny resemblance to the legendarily inept character Barney Fife on *The Andy Griffith Show.*

All of this was totally unnecessary. Colton said, "Fellas, I'm just going to buy new tires to put on it."

"That's all fine and good but seeing as how you're a potential witness, we're going to need to ask you some questions."

Then they'd make it damn fast because he only had a finite amount of time with Andi and was going to make damn sure every minute counted.

ANDI ROLLED OVER onto her stomach, a satisfied smile curving her lips. Colton felt the same way. While life might hold many uncertainties, whether they were sexually compatible was no longer on that particular list. They were. In spades. Making love with her just got better and better.

"I hesitate to say this," she said, running her fingers down his arm, eliciting a response inside him even though he was spent. "Because you'll think all I ever think about is food—"

He grinned like the happy fool he was. "No, honey. I can attest food is not the only thing on your mind."

She nudged him playfully. "As I was saying, or rather about to say, I'm hungry."

He was finding her playfulness brought out a measure of the same he hadn't known he possessed.

"Well, I believe our dining choices are the truck stop, the truck stop or the truck stop."

"Then why don't we walk over and dine at the truck stop?" Her smile was infectious.

"Just a suggestion, but you may want to put on some clothes first."

She feigned shock. "You think?"

"I'm fine with you that way but I really don't want to fight today and I'm pretty sure one would break out and then there's the matter of having to bail you out of jail. But you'll be on your own explaining the public-nudity charge to your mother."

She rolled to her side and swung her legs over the bed's edge, sitting up. "Damn. You really know how to kill a party. I guess I'll get dressed before we go."

Colton needed to dress as well but he sat back and watched her move naked across the room, enjoying the bounce of her backside and the sway of her breasts—which were magnificent. She stepped into a pair of black panties and reached for her bra, when she looked up and saw him still sitting on the bed. "Aren't you planning to get dressed too, Major?" She clapped her hands in a let's-get-on-with-it manner. "I'm starving here."

He grinned. She did have an appetite—in every respect. "In a minute."

"Are you watching me?"

"Yes, ma'am, I am and I'm telling you the pleasure is mine."

"Alrighty, then," she said, continuing to dress. It didn't take long. She walked over to the bed and grabbed his hand. "Now your turn," she said, tugging at him.

"Okay. You're a demanding woman," he said, laughing as he rose to his feet.

She plopped onto the spot he'd just vacated on the bed. "Now I'm going to watch." She pursed her lips and turned her head from side to side as if trying to make a decision as he pulled on his BVDs. "You know, I really, really like you in your uniform." He stepped into his jeans. "You look so distinguished." He pulled on his shirt. "And those jeans and shirt are a good look as well but when it comes down to it, I think I prefer you naked."

"Odd, I was thinking the same about you."

"Hey, you're the one who asked me to put on clothes."

"No worries, honey, I'll address that when we get back from eating." He tucked his shirt into his pants and fastened the belt.

She hopped off of the bed. "Okay, let's roll. Hold on a sec." She ducked into the bathroom and dragged her brush through her hair. Walking back into the bedroom, she put it on the dresser. "Okay, now I don't look as if I just rolled out of bed."

"Except your lips are swollen and I did get a little

carried away there." He pointed to her neck and then the edge of her right breast. "Damn, and there, too. I didn't realize you had such delicate skin. I'll be more careful."

She looked at him, suddenly serious, her teasing vanished. "No. This morning and this afternoon were great, incredible, and I don't want you to change anything or hold back. We have three days together and I want us to make the most of them and that doesn't include you being careful because you might leave a mark on my skin."

He didn't want to hold back with her. "If that's how you want it."

"That's definitely how I want it."

They stepped out into the late-afternoon sun. Since he wasn't holding back, he reached between them and caught her hand up in his. They walked down the sidewalk running the front of the motel holding hands. Burt and Vernette were sitting in the front office watching television and didn't look up as they passed, which was just as well considering what was sure to be a lengthy conversation, on their part, would have ensued.

They stood at the edge of the three-lane highway separating The Daisy from the truck stop. Only a few cars sat in the truck-stop parking lot but several big rigs were lined up on the blacktop across the street.

They entered the restaurant and settled in a booth

that offered a scenic view of the parking lot, highway and the near end of The Daisy Inn.

Andi looked over the menu. "Wow, I should really have a salad but that country fried steak with mashed potatoes and gravy with fried okra looks good."

Colton shook his head. "Order what you really want. You just burned a lot of calories…and you're going to burn more."

Their waitress, who was definitely not nearly as friendly or outgoing as Rochelle at the Waffle House had been, came over with water glasses. "Y'all know what you want?"

Colton glanced across at Andi for her to order first. She ordered the country fried steak with all the trimmings and a sweet tea. "I'll have the same," Colton said.

Their waitress walked away and Colton looked at Andi across the booth. "You really are a Southern girl, aren't you?"

A strange look crossed her face which he couldn't quite define. "What I really am is a girl from the South."

"Explain."

"I love my heritage and where I'm from, but it's stifling me. I don't think I realized until I climbed out of the window and we were on the expressway just how trapped I've felt and not by just the upcoming marriage and Blanton, but by everything." She turned her head to stare out the window. "When I said I didn't want to go back yesterday, it wasn't just because I didn't want to face my family and friends. I didn't want to go back because I wanted to go somewhere else and see something else and do something else." She redirected her gaze back to him. "Do you understand what I'm saying?"

He'd never felt stifled but then his parents had been vastly different from her mother. "To some extent. I knew I wanted to be in the military from the time I was a kid, but I can't say I ever felt trapped."

"Colton, my future's been mapped out by my mother since I was old enough to walk and talk. I've always known what was expected of me because I've been told all my life. I'm going to marry well, produce grandchildren, teach Sunday school and take care of my mother when the time comes. That's what good Southern girls do. And once Rion left for the military, it was a thousand times worse. Duty and obligation are the hallmark of my existence."

He'd seen it for years. "I know how your mother can be."

"I want to see this country, the world. I want different experiences." He could understand that. He'd known he didn't want to stay in Savannah. "Every time I talked about traveling or taking a trip with my former roommate, my mother guilted me into not taking it. There was always some reason it would be a bad time for me to go, and it was always backed up by how worried sick about me she'd be the whole time."

"Have you tried telling her how you feel?"

"Yes. I talked to her about it. Once a week she invited me out to dinner. The first week we went to a Mexican restaurant where a mariachi band walked around from table to table playing. The next week it was Italian food. I forget the particular lineup after that but we covered Indian, Thai, Chinese, Irish and she even found a little German deli. Oh, yeah, and there was a Vietnamese restaurant and a Jewish deli. That was her solution to me wanting to live somewhere else."

Damn. Colton didn't quite know what to say. He knew firsthand what Rion had gone through with his mother when he'd made the decision to join the military. It hadn't been pretty. Daisy had disintegrated all over again. Rion's love for his family had been questioned numerous times. He'd repeatedly assured his mother he loved her but wouldn't have his life dictated by her.

Colton knew without a doubt it would be much worse on Andi because she was female. He wasn't sexist, but he knew how her mother thought. But Andi had the right to live her life the way she wanted to.

In his own way he had played into Daisy's control because Colton had been very much aware if he and Andi had any kind of future it would cause a horrible rift between her and her mother.

He said the only thing he knew to say. "Our parents have all had their own lives to live. They made their own choices. You know, when we're children it's their job to guide us, but once we're adults, our lives are our own to live."

Their waitress returned with laden plates. "Y'all need anything else right now?"

Neither of them did and she left them alone once again. Andi shrugged self-consciously. "Sorry. I didn't mean for that to turn into a dumpfest."

"That wasn't a dumpfest. That's what you call a real conversation between two friends. We grew up together. I spent half my childhood and adolescence at your house. I know your mother. If you can't talk to me about this, then who can you talk to? I just wish there was something I could do."

Her smile tore at his heart. "The doing's all on me." She drew a deep breath. "When we get back I'm telling her I'm not staying. She's already going to be upset with me so I might as well get it all out at once. And I'd be lying if I didn't say that I'm scared to death she's going to have another breakdown, but I can't continue to live my life for her." She cut her steak into bite-size pieces.

"It'll be tough for a while but she still loves Rion, doesn't she? She'll still love you when the dust settles. And you know my mother will be there for her."

"But she'll hate you." She seemed to catch herself, as if she hadn't meant to be so blunt. "Sorry, but she's resented you ever since you and Rion left home."

He shrugged. "That's nothing I haven't known."

She worried her lower lip with her teeth. "Maybe I should wait a couple of weeks or even months until after you leave to bring it up. Otherwise she'll definitely blame you for this."

He was shaking his head before the last word left her mouth. He'd stand in the line of fire for her any day. "No. If you're sure, then move forward with your plans. Where do you think you want to go?"

"I've always been intrigued by Boston and New York. I know they're both wickedly expensive but if I'm going to go for it, I'm going to really go for it. I'll need to research the cost of living in several places before I decide." She shook her head. "I know I won't be staying at home long, though. I'll move back out temporarily until I decide."

"I can help you gather statistics on Boston and New York. I'm good at research."

Much as she had with Rion, Daisy would want someone to blame other than her child, and once again, it would be Colton. When all of this was said and done, Daisy Mitchell would forever hate him.

WHEN THE KNOCK SOUNDED on the back door, Martha Anne put her issue of *Southern Living* on the end table and took off her reading glass. It had to be Daisy. Anyone else who came calling on a Sunday evening would go to the front door.

There'd been a time, when they'd first moved into the neighborhood in the early eighties, when she'd never locked her back door, but not now. Those days were long gone. She checked the curtain over the half-window. Sure enough Daisy stood on the other side. Martha Anne unlocked the door and invited her in.

When she came into the house it was apparent she'd been crying. Red rimmed her eyes and her nose was swollen. She clutched a tissue in her hand.

Closing the back door behind her, panic threatened Martha Anne. "What's the matter? What's wrong?"

"I'm worried sick, that's what's wrong," Daisy said.

Her panic subsided. If it was something truly horrible, Daisy would've blurted it out. Martha Anne put her arm around Daisy's shoulders and led her into the den, to the love seat. She settled her friend there and took a seat in the opposite chair. "Over what? What are you worried sick over?"

"I haven't heard from Andi all day and she's not answering her cell phone."

This she could handle. It was simply more of Daisy's neurosis. "I'm sure she's fine."

Miserable, Daisy shook her head, dabbing at her eyes with the tissue. "I'm sure she's not."

"Why in the world would you think that?"

She looked at Martha Anne as if she were missing what was painfully obvious. "It's been more than twenty-four hours since I heard from her."

Andi had made it clear on the phone when they'd

spoken yesterday that she needed some time away. "That's because she's taking a little vacation and that includes a vacation from you, from all of us."

"But she's never—"

Martha Anne cut her off, knowing precisely where she was going with this. "She's never had the chance, has she? When Mattie moved out, sometimes we only talked once a week," Martha Anne pointed out. "She was busy with her life and I was busy with mine. That's the way it's supposed to be with our children who've all grown up now. They have their own lives."

"What if they had an accident?"

She knew exactly what was driving Daisy's obsessive worry. She didn't need a psychology degree to know her experience with losing Gerald the way she had was driving this now, had been driving it for years, but Daisy had to get a grip. Martha Anne tried laying out the circumstances as logically as she could. "There's not a doubt in my mind they've not had an accident but, on the extremely rare chance they did, if Colton was even semiconscious he would contact me. If he was unconscious then either the police or the hospital would've called by now since the registration and insurance papers in the glove box list this address and my phone number is attached to this address."

She quit wringing her hands in her lap. "You really think they're okay?"

"I'm sure they're okay."

"But when Gerald—"

Exasperation warred with sympathy inside her. "Daisy, I know that was hard. It was hard for me to lose Allen and I wasn't left with two small children to raise alone, mine were older, so I can't imagine what that was like. But you have got to come to grips."

Daisy tightened her lips. "When I do hear from her, I'm going to let her know what I think of her worrying me this way. I've been frantic this afternoon."

It was time to be blunt. "And that's not Andi's fault, that's your fault. You're the one who chooses to worry. It's a choice you're making. Give your daughter some room to live her life."

"I want her to be happy, but I want her to be safe."

"Of course you do, we all want that for our children. But right up under you doesn't necessarily mean she's safe. She's taking a couple of days away to get her head together."

"I don't want to be this way, Martha Anne, I just can't seem to help it."

Martha Anne believed her. It was as if Daisy's neurotic side took over and stripped away all rationale. "I'm only telling you this because you're my friend and I love you but instead of getting better, you're getting worse." It was like looking at someone you saw every day. She hadn't really paid attention to the fact Daisy was gradually getting worse and worse. But it was apparent. And even if it impacted their friendship, she had to say what she was about to say. "I think you need to see a therapist."

Daisy whipped her head up. "What? So someone can poke around in my life and my brain?" She crossed her arms over her chest, a mutinous look on her face.

Martha Anne went and sat on the love seat next to her friend. "No, so someone can help you work through this." She put her arm around Daisy's shoulder and squeezed. "Do you really think you're the only person with this issue? Of course you're not. A therapist can help you put practical coping mechanisms into place."

Daisy teared up and rested her head in her hands. "I want my children to love me."

"They do love you, but they don't have to be glued to your side to love you, Daisy. I can ask around at school for the name of a good therapist." She cut her friend off at the pass before she could even give it voice. "And no one needs to know who it's for or what it's about."

For the longest few seconds, Daisy simply sat there, obviously weighing her choices. Finally she nodded. "Would you come with me? Just to the first appointment?"

"Of course I will. That's what friends are for."

12

"Y'ALL TAKE CARE AND don't forget to drop us a note now and then to let us know how you're doing," Vernette yelled, as they backed out and pulled away from The Daisy Inn late Monday morning.

"Will do," Andi yelled back as they made a left-hand turn to access the interstate. She felt oddly nostalgic leaving the quaint inn and the couple who were obviously still in love and devoted to one another after more than fifty years together. When she looked at Vernette and Burt Pickle it made her ache inside because that's what she wanted with Colton. She'd started this thinking being with him would help her get over him but she was more than aware there'd never be any getting over Colton. She'd realized she was a one-man woman and that man was Major Colton Sawyer.

"Now exactly how is that going to work?" Colton asked, quirking an eyebrow in her direction.

Sometimes Major Logical Reasoning totally missed things. "She gave me their address."

"I know how the writing a note works." He all but rolled his eyes at her. Lucky for him she found him endearing. "I mean they think we're married."

Andi shrugged. "So, I'll update them on you and update them on me and they don't have to know we're not together. It's sort of funny how so many people have assumed we're married on this trip." Too bad he didn't seem to be taking the hint. Didn't he realize by now they belonged together?

"I think we can safely assume it's the big white dress hanging in the backseat and the rock on your finger that's giving that impression."

Apparently not. But she refused to give up. Andi was not a quitter so instead of bonking him on the head the way she wanted to—not to mention that wasn't safe when he was the one driving—she grinned and offered him information he could relate to: the logic behind her still wearing her engagement ring. "The safest place for this rock, as you put it, until I can return it to Blanton, is on my finger. He wasn't cheap and I don't want to lose it and have to buy it off him. That'd put a major dent in my savings. And maybe the ring and dress have a smidgen to do with it but I think it's the way you gaze at me all starry-eyed." Put that in your pipe and smoke it, Major.

"And here I thought it was you who was gazing at me all starry-eyed."

This was yet another memory in the making. She didn't think he'd ever actually flirted with her before. "In your dreams, Major."

"Backatcha."

"Seriously—"

"I thought you were being serious."

She couldn't seem to help herself. She had to ask. "Do you ever think about getting married?"

"No." She wished she hadn't asked. "The military is hard on families. I knew that going in. I can volunteer for assignments and know if things go wrong, I'm not leaving a family behind without a husband or father."

"But what if you care for someone and they care for you? Does it hurt any less to lose you if you're not married than if you are?"

"Yes, it does. If you care for someone, you simply care for them. Being married involves plans for the future and all of that dies with that person." She shuddered. "Sorry, Andi, but death and dealing with death are part of the realities of a soldier in wartime. It's a very real part of my world, your brother's world."

The sun was suddenly less bright. She felt like crying. The thought of anything happening to Colton or Rion was nearly unbearable. It wasn't as if she hadn't thought about it before but somehow it seemed so much more real and tangible now that he'd brought it out onto the table, now that she was sitting next to him, now that they'd made love. "I get that. I'm sorry

I brought it up. This is your leave and I'm sure that's not what you want to think about or talk about."

"Andi, it's like I told you over dinner last night, we'll talk about whatever you want to talk about or need to talk about."

She didn't want to talk about him not wanting to tie anyone to him and she certainly didn't want to talk about losing either him or her brother. She determinedly changed the subject, having had lots of practice with her mother on keeping things on an even keel. "Okay, then let's talk about what we want to do when we get to Gatlinburg." When it came right down to it, she didn't know what kind of stuff he liked to do. Did they like the same things? What was his idea of a good time? Well, she knew both their idea of a good time in the bedroom but…

"Give me the rundown on our choices once we get there."

She thought back to things she'd heard about the area over the years. "Let's see, there's hiking, horseback riding, although I'm a little saddle sore so I'd rather skip that, there's lots of shops and restaurants, and there are even a few wedding chapels—"

"Wedding chapels?" Colton laughed. "Do they supply the groom? 'Cause I'm going to be waiting outside the bathroom window again."

Ouch. She'd thrown that in there because she couldn't seem to help herself today. And he'd just made it abundantly clear he had no intention of being the groom. She forced a smile through her hurt. "It would make a good story. I've got the dress. How many women could say they ditched two weddings in one week?"

"With different grooms nonetheless."

"That'd certainly be different if the same guy showed up to be stood up twice."

"He'd need his head examined."

She agreed although stranger things had happened. "Hey, you hear about people all the time who marry, divorce and marry again."

Colton shook his head. "That's just weird. You either work it out or you don't. You're wedding obsessed."

No, she wasn't. She was Colton Sawyer obsessed but he could think what he wanted. Andi laughed. "It's the dress in the backseat. I'm just teasing you. We'll strike the wedding chapel. No horseback riding and no weddings."

"Aiding and abetting you in one escape per week is plenty."

She realized how content she was to be driving along the expressway with him, having this inane conversation. "A good accomplice is a rare commodity."

"Hey, I'm driving now, aren't I? Are we not on the road to Gatlinburg, the ultimate destination in this Grand Adventure of yours?"

The idea struck her that it wasn't a matter of the

destination that made it a Grand Adventure. It was all about the journey. "Just how attached are you to the idea of going to Gatlinburg?" she asked him.

He slanted a questioning look her way. "I'm only attached in the sense that you wanted a Grand Adventure and that's where you said you wanted to go."

"Well, I did want a Grand Adventure and this has been but a couple of things have changed. I'm not going to stay in Savannah now so that sort of makes a difference. And the other, which is really the biggie, is when I decided I wanted to go to Gatlinburg, spending time in bed with you wasn't a viable option. Now that it is, spending all these hours in the car driving when we could be spending all these hours in the bed before we have to go back, well, it just seems like a waste."

"Let me get this straight, you don't want to go to Gatlinburg because you don't want to spend the drive time when we could be in bed together?"

There was no point in being less than honest about it. They didn't have time to waste. "Yeah. We've only got a couple of days. You're leaving Friday. I don't want to waste that time. What do you think?"

He grinned. "I think that's a good answer. So, where do you want to go?"

"I sort of have a soft spot for that room at The Daisy. And it's not that far to drive back to Savannah from there, unless you're concerned the tires might get ripped off again."

"No, it's probably one of the safest places to park now. Those kids won't show up again anytime soon. Burt and Vernette would be thrilled. Let's see, driving several more hours and then driving back on Wednesday or spending that time horizontal with you? That's a tough call." He pretended to ponder the situation. "Andi, I'm fine with The Daisy if you're sure you don't want to go to Gatlinburg."

He might not want her for forever, but it was reassuring that he wanted as much of her as possible until he left on Friday. "I'm positive. And I hope you don't think I'm a flake—first running out on a wedding and now changing my mind about this, but sometimes you just have to adapt as the situation changes."

"I don't think you're a flake. There's one thing you learn early on and that's the situation dictates. You have to have a plan but when the circumstances or situation changes you have to be able to adapt your plans to those changes. And I understand you climbing out that window."

She had the oddest sense he did, simply because he knew her family better than anyone else did. "Do you really?"

"Yeah, I understand what you were up against."

She knew he was referring to her mother. It was great to be with someone who "got" her, who understood where she was coming from. She pointed to the green interstate sign slightly ahead. "There's an exit in a mile and a half. We can turn around there."

THURSDAY MORNING Colton awoke instantly, the result of years of military conditioning where a drowsy state could mean a dead state. Andi was curled up next to him, her head on his right arm, his left wrapped around her. That was the way she liked to sleep.

He was used to sleeping alone and unused to sharing a bed with anyone. He had adapted to it quickly though. He liked waking up to her hair tickling his face, her buttocks pressed against his crotch, her breasts beneath his forearm and hand.

She was an even more amazing woman than he'd ever realized. It was as if they'd crammed weeks of dating and sex into the few days available to them. They'd fallen into the routine of making love first thing in the morning and then setting out to explore the surrounding area. They'd checked out two antiques stores in the neighboring town, afterward sitting in the park eating ice cream from a small, old-fashioned soda shop. Andi's favorite ice-cream choice was vanilla with hot chocolate sauce on top, complete with whipped cream and a cherry. One afternoon they'd gone to the local Cineplex where they'd shared hot buttered popcorn, a drink and the latest suspense release. And then yesterday the bottom had fallen out and it had rained like hell all day. They'd called a local pizza-delivery joint and spent the day in bed eating pizza, reading, talking and making love.

Over the course of the past few days they'd logged hours talking. They'd discovered they both believed in ghosts, though neither felt any ghostly presence at The Daisy. Andi had a real grasp on politics and current events. They'd covered the gamut of everything from immigration to educational policies.

They didn't always agree but she was well-informed and she wasn't intractable, two qualities he admired. She wasn't shy about embracing an opposing view and he had to admire that, as well. He relished a discussion where his opinion was challenged yet respected.

One of the things he'd never realized over the years was just how smart and well-rounded Andi was. And she was damn fun. He hadn't realized just how much spontaneity was missing from his life. An impromptu road trip simply wasn't in his repertoire.

He looked at her in the bed next to him. Tomorrow morning they'd wake up in separate beds, separate houses. This was the last time he'd be privy to having her in his bed, her hair splayed out over the pillow, her hand tucked beneath the curve of her cheek.

Yes, it had been a helluva week. She could play a mean hand of poker and last, but definitely not least, they were incredibly sexually compatible. The edible panties were gone. The fur-covered handcuffs had been tried out, amidst much laughter, and they'd each cashed in a few of the naughty coupons Vernette had included in their basket.

Leaving Andi to go back—hell, leaving Andi period—was going to be one of the hardest things he'd ever done. No, make that the single hardest thing he'd ever done. But one of Colton's father's favorite sayings, picked up from *his* father, had always been *the right thing to do isn't always the easy thing to do.*

So, while walking away from her, leaving her free to move on with her life wasn't the easy thing to do, it was the right thing to do. She'd made a huge decision in deciding to move away from Savannah and see some of the world. He had a feeling her artistic endeavors were going to blossom wherever she wound up, whether it was Boston or New York. He didn't think it would be particularly easy for her, but his Andi had grit and determination in spades, otherwise she'd have never survived all these years with Daisy and she'd have never climbed out that window in the first damn place.

She stirred next to him, blinking her eyes open, a lazy just-waking-up smile curving her lips and lighting her eyes. He loved the way she looked at him, as if his presence alone was enough to make her happy. He loved it, but it simultaneously scared the hell out of him. He'd seen firsthand what losing Gerald had done to Daisy, how his father's heart attack and subsequent death had affected his mother, and then the men who'd been lost to war and left behind widows and fatherless children. He pushed aside the melancholy thought and brought himself firmly back to the here and now.

"Morning, sleepyhead." He smoothed her hair back from her cheek.

She reached up and caught his hand in hers, bringing it to her lips to press a kiss to his fingers. "Good morning."

From that moment, they moved into the silent dance which had become their morning lovemaking. Today, this morning, however, they were both aware that this was their last time together. They'd return to Savannah. Tomorrow he'd be headed back to his assignment.

Colton was nearly desperate as he rolled her to her belly and kissed his way down her neck, the indent of her spine, the curve of her back, the flare of her hips, the sensitive backs of her knees, even the delicate lines of her ankles. The texture of her skin, her taste against his tongue, her scent, the mapping of the curves and undulations of her body—these were all things his logical mind sought to commit to memory for the impending time when memory would have to suffice. These alone would have to be enough in the upcoming weeks, months and years. It would have to be enough that Andi had been his for this short period of time and he would forever carry with him this intimate knowledge of her.

She sighed into the silence as he turned her to her back with a gentle pressure on her hip. He slid up her beautiful body and she welcomed him with open arms and open legs. Sliding her arms around his neck, she said, "Colton, I—"

He kissed her, cutting her off. As surely as he knew his own name, he knew she was about to declare her love for him. He knew how she felt about him. He knew it every time she held his hand, every time she welcomed him into her body. And surely she knew he loved her, as well. It imbued every facet of his interaction with her. But, somehow, saying it, declaring it, changed everything. With a spoken declaration, it wouldn't be nearly as easy to walk away…and in the end that was what he needed to do.

So, he kissed her, saying in the kiss what he couldn't and wouldn't put into words. And as the kisses deepened and became more intense, he put everything he had into making love to her one last time.

13

HOURS LATER, Andi stared out the window. It was quiet in the car between them as the Buick ate up the miles on the interstate, relentlessly narrowing the amount of time they had together, sending them back to their families and the realities of their obligations and day-to-day life. It was as if the fairy tale that had been the two of them together faded with each roll of the tires on the asphalt.

Every fiber of her being rebelled at the notion of giving up her time with him, of returning to whatever they'd been to one another before. Although Colton sat right next to her, she could feel his steady withdrawal, his retreat from her with each mile that passed.

"So what's the game plan?" she finally said. "Do we pretend that none of this happened between us?"

"It's really no one's business."

That wasn't what she meant. "It's our business and

I'm talking about between us. This has changed everything. I think we thought it wouldn't, but being the people we are, it has." That sounded slightly convoluted, but she thought he knew what she meant. There was nothing casual about him and there was nothing casual about her. "I can't go back to what we were before, which was essentially strangers who grew up next to one another."

"I don't want that, either," Colton said quietly. "I'll give you my email and we can stay in touch."

She knew she was going against every "rule" of dating and relationships. According to the rules she wasn't supposed to make herself too available. She was supposed to make him chase her, pursue her. And those dating rules might work with most men, but Colton wasn't most men. He wouldn't chase. And those rules were bogus anyway when she considered he could very well be dead next week. A woman didn't play games and follow silly rules with a man who was in a war. The stakes were too high.

She loved him. It wasn't a girlish crush. It wasn't the manifestation of a physical relationship. From the moment she'd accepted Blanton's proposal she'd known a tension inside, a sense of foreboding that had increased the closer the wedding got. And that was because her heart was already spoken for. Somewhere in the back of her psyche she'd known he wasn't the man for her. Perhaps because she knew he wasn't the man Colton was. No one would ever be Colton, no one else would ever measure up to him.

"That's not going to be enough," she said.

Startled, he glanced over at her. "What?"

"I said, that's not going to be enough." Maybe her timing was bad considering he was driving, but then again, maybe her timing was perfect since he was essentially a captive audience and had to hear her out. "I love you. I think I have for a long time, so emailing isn't going to be nearly enough."

He was already shaking his head. "Andi, we talked about your situation. You're on the rebound—"

She laughed. "I am not on the rebound. And it's not as if Blanton is the one who dumped me or left me at the altar, if you'll recall. And I know you care for me or you would've never slept with me because you're not a casual-sex kind of guy. And I'm not a casual-sex kind of woman." She thought of her brother and several of her close friends and felt beholden to tack on "Not that I think there's anything wrong with that, but it's just not either one of us."

"Andi, I do care about you, but you knew going into this what I could offer."

"You're shortchanging both of us. We're still in South Carolina. They don't require a blood test. We could stop and get married on the way home. Or we could pick up the paperwork and come back tomorrow if you wanted to bring our families."

"Everything else aside, what do you think your

mother would have to say about the two of us getting married? There's already her resentment over Rion—"

"Unfounded."

"But real nonetheless. And I'm certain I've secured my spot at the top of her shit list by helping you leave the wedding and then being gone with you for four days…and nights. And we both know I'm going to be at fault when you tell her you've decided to move."

This was all true enough. And at least she had him talking about getting married, even if it was in the hypothetical sense and he was arguing against it. "So how much worse can it get if we were married?"

"Oh, it could and it would. She won't be happy about you striking out on your own, but she'll cling to the hope you won't like it or will simply be so homesick you'll return to Savannah soon enough."

Now that she'd finally made up her mind, she was resolute. "I won't."

"I don't think you will either, but she'll convince herself because it's going to be all she has to hold on to. But if you married me she wouldn't have that hope anymore. I'll never be stationed near here. So, it would be much, much worse."

"When I climbed out that window, it was a turning point for me. I think I realized then and there I was done making decisions based on what my mother wanted. I want her to be well, I want her to be mentally healthy but I can't be responsible for her mental health. And if I wasn't willing to marry a man I didn't love to please her, I'm certainly not willing to give up a man I do love to please her."

His profile could've been cast in stone. "I've told you how I feel about marriage and my career."

It stung that he had yet to acknowledge that she'd said she loved him, not just once, but twice now.

"And I'm sorry but it doesn't make any sense. Look at our fathers. A freak accident took mine and a heart attack claimed yours. What? According to your rationale, no one should get married because eventually one person is guaranteed to lose the other one."

"But neither of our mothers lived with the day-to-day uncertainty. Is today the day an IED tears my husband apart? Is today the day a sniper's bullet finds him? If he comes back, will he be missing parts? Will he be the same man who left, because most of us aren't? How will we adapt to living together again?"

She wasn't naive. She didn't think it would be easy to live with that uncertainty, but she'd rather live with the uncertainty than live without him. "I'm willing to take that chance. I want to make plans with you. I want us to build a future. I want us to grow old together, and if that time is cut short, I'll be thankful for the time I have you."

"Andi, we had a great time together but you're young and you'll meet someone else—"

She cut him off because if he finished, her head

might just explode on her shoulders. "Stop. Stop right there. Don't you dare patronize me. There will never be anyone else. I think from the time I've been ten years old, you ruined me for any other man. I'll never find someone else because someone else won't be you. Do not even begin to trivialize what I feel for you by saying that, ever again."

"Fine."

He wasn't happy with her for having her say but that was okay because she wasn't particularly happy with him either. The terse silence stretched between them, the only sound the hum of the tires over the blacktop. She replayed previous conversations in her mind and it clicked for her. He might not say it, he might not tell her what she wanted to hear, but she *knew*.

"I'm the one, aren't I? I'm the one who was never available and in your crazy way of looking at things you're still keeping me unavailable."

He said nothing, just continued to stare straight ahead as he drove.

COLTON PULLED INTO his mother's driveway and killed the engine. He and Andi had discussed much of nothing the rest of the way home, but their earlier conversation had hung there between them.

"I'll get my dress later," Andi said.

He had come so close to telling her how he felt about her in the car, but it would've simply made her more dogmatic and resolved. And hearing her tell him not once, but twice that she loved him had been bittersweet. He needed some time away from her, some time to think. Of course, he was about to have that in spades when he left tomorrow morning.

"You want me to carry it over?" he offered on the dress. In a moment of rare irrationality he didn't want to see her cross that yard, swallowed by the sameness of their past. But hadn't he just told her that was precisely what he wanted? But he also didn't want to send her in there to face Daisy alone. "You want me there when you talk to—"

She cut him off. "No. I need to talk to my mother alone."

"Are you sure? I'll go with you."

"Thank you, I appreciate the offer, but I have to do this alone." He doubted she was even aware she stood a little taller and straighter when she said that. "And I don't want her jumping on your case if you walk in with the dress. It's sat in the car since Saturday. It can sit in the car a little longer. I will warn you, though, I'm going to tell her how I feel about you."

"Why?"

"First, because it's very real. Second, because I want her to know that I'd follow you to the ends of the earth, but you won't let me." She took her suitcase out of the trunk and smiled but it was full of melancholy. "It was a Grand Adventure, wasn't it?"

"It was that." He stood stock still, next to his door, by the path that led to her mother's house.

She rounded the rear of the car and paused next to him. Reaching up, she caressed his jaw with her fingers. "We could have lots more times like that." She dropped her hand to her side. "I'll see you."

"Good luck with your news. Call me if you need reinforcements."

"Thanks, but I'm a big girl, I can handle it."

He nodded. "I know you can."

She crossed the lawn, following the path he and Rion had worn years before, going back and forth, a path their mothers still trod.

He was pulling his bag out of the trunk when the kitchen door opened and his mother came out into the garage, which might as well have been a carport since no one ever bothered to close the garage doors. "I thought I heard a car door."

He closed the trunk and crossed to where she stood waiting. He gave her a one-armed hug. "How are you, Mom?"

"Fine. Glad to see my son again," she said with a smile to make sure there was no sting behind it. He followed her into the house. "Did you have a good trip?"

"Yeah, I did," he said as he walked down the hall to deposit his bag in the guest room. He returned to the kitchen and propped against the door frame. "There was one little incident." He relayed the story about the tires being stolen without going into detail regarding the circumstances. "So, the car now has new tires."

"I'll look at them when I get this in the oven," she said as she mixed egg, ground beef and seasoned breadcrumbs for a meat loaf. She was making that for him before he had to go back tomorrow. Meat loaf and mashed potatoes were one of his favorite meals. "I'll pay you back for them."

She shaped the seasoned meat into a ring in a square pan, the same pan she'd used for meat loaf for as long as he could remember. "No way," he said, checking her on paying for the tires. "I took off in the car, it was in my care when it happened and I can easily afford it."

After popping the meat loaf into the oven, she started peeling potatoes. He could easily head to his room, but for some strange reason he felt a need he hadn't in years—to spend time with his mother. "Need any help with that?" he offered.

"No, but you can keep me company."

He poured himself a glass of iced tea and then settled on one of the bar stools at the counter. "Look, Mom, there's something you should know."

She looked up from peeling the spuds with a big, happy smile. "Son, it's all over your face and I'm fine with it. Mattie guessed. It'll take Daisy a while to come around, but she will. I'm personally thrilled. I've always liked Andi. I did witness that little exchange in the driveway. And not to be pushy but I want to go on record as saying I'd rather have grand-children sooner than later. And you know, you're not exactly getting any younger."

What the hell? "You're way off base," he said. Technically, she wasn't but that wasn't the issue they needed to discuss. "I'm telling you this, not to tell you Andi's news, but because you'll be the one fielding the fallout. Andi's leaving Savannah."

She nodded. "But of course she is if you're—"

Sometimes his mother only heard what she wanted to hear. "Mom, slow down and listen. Her leaving Savannah has nothing to do with me."

His mother paused in the potato peeling, a frown drawing her eyebrows together over the tops of her glasses. "How can that be? She's not moving to Natick?"

"No. She's striking out on her own."

"Alone?"

"Alone."

"But why? What happened to the two of you?" She looked at him sharply with a faint edge of maternal disapproval, as if this was his fault.

"There is no us."

"I'm confused."

He could understand that. She was beginning to confuse even him, and he knew what was going on. "It's sort of complicated. Andi decided on this trip she's leaving Savannah. Apparently she's been trying to talk to Daisy about it for a while and Daisy just won't hear it."

"Where's she going?"

"Either New York or Boston."

"Mercy." His mother paused, peeler in hand, and leaned against the work island. "You know Daisy's going to fall apart and she's going to blame you for this."

"I know. I didn't have anything to do with it, but I know she'll blame me."

Resuming the task at hand, she threw a seemingly innocuous question his way. "Colton, why didn't you want to stay for Andi's reception on Saturday?"

He damn sure didn't like where this was heading. "I don't like weddings."

His mother didn't buy a minute of it. "I never noticed that before."

"Don't make a big deal out of nothing."

"Do you know I'm the one who asked your daddy to marry me?" She added water to the potatoes in the pot and set it aside.

That was news to him. "How is it that I'm thirty-two and just now hearing this?"

"Because things were different back when we were dating, thirty-six years ago. Nowadays young women don't think a thing about asking a man out, but that's not how things were done in my day. And asking a man to marry you…well, it wasn't anything Allen or

I ever wanted to advertise since it didn't particularly reflect well for either one of us for our day in time."

Opening the refrigerator, she pulled out a bag of fresh carrots and a container of fresh green beans. He loved her gingered carrots. She really was pulling out all the stops for him.

"Why did you feel you had to ask him?"

She looked at him as if he had missed the obvious. "Because I loved him and I was pretty sure he loved me, but he wouldn't ask me. Apparently you Sawyer men require some nudging. It turns out both your grandmother and your great-grandmother had to step up to the plate as well…and it certainly was unheard of in their day."

"And you know this how?"

"Women used to keep diaries and journals. Your aunt Margaret—" that was his father's older sister "—shared her mother's and grandmother's diaries with me a couple of years ago."

"And you're telling me this why?"

"Because I thought you needed to know."

Well, while they were dragging all of this out, he might as well tell her the other news Andi was going to break to Daisy because Daisy'd be sure to bring that up to his mother, as well.

"There is another conversation Andi's going to have with her mother which will probably make its way back to you, as well."

"Why do I have the feeling this is going to be even better than her other bit of news?"

He didn't see any good way to ease into this so he simply threw it out there. "Andi says she's in love with me."

His mother looked triumphant. "Ah-ha. So we were right. I'm telling you it was your sister who figured it out." She paused. "So then why isn't she moving to Natick? I'm confused again."

"Mom, she was supposed to marry Blanton less than a week ago. And now she's in love with me? All this time and she never gave me any inkling, any sign?"

"Did you ever let her know how you felt?"

"Well, no," he answered automatically…and then realized what he'd said.

Across the expanse of Formica, his mother looked smug. She'd been tricky and he'd fallen right into that.

"No worries. We'll get it all sorted out over dinner. I talked to Daisy earlier today. Andi and Daisy are joining us for your farewell dinner this evening." She paused in midcarrot scrape. "Hold that thought," she said as she put down the vegetable and utensil and rinsed her hands in the sink. Drying them on her apron, she bustled off to her bedroom. She returned within a few minutes and dropped a velveteen box on the counter in front of him.

She'd gone and gotten the ring. Inside was a ruby

that had been handed down for generations by the Sawyer men to their intended. His great-great-grand-father or perhaps it was his great-great-great-grand-father, he always forgot just how far removed he was in the line of greats. But anyway, his name had been Orin Sawyer and he'd won the ruby ring in a poker game. It had been handed down subsequently as a sign of devotion to the wife of the oldest Sawyer son.

"I don't need that, Mom."

"We'll see, we'll see." She reached over and patted his hand. "Just hold on to it."

14

ANDI HEADED FOR the shower. She could hear her mother crying in the other room. That had gone just as badly as she'd anticipated. Much as with when her brother was leaving for the military, her mother had taken her decision to move as not a sign of independence but as a severing. She didn't see how Andi could leave her if she loved her. It had been a repeat of the same tapes she'd played for years.

Andi did know that, as had happened with Rion, her mother still loved her and would eventually come around. She had, however, reacted precisely as Andi had known she would when Andi brought up her feelings for Colton. And Andi had had a huge epiphany. Her mother only wanted Andi's happiness on her mother's terms.

Things would eventually sort out with her mother. Andi'd been infinitely relieved to hear her mother say Martha Anne had talked her into seeing a therapist and was going to go with her. Of course, it had been thrown out there as an inducement for Andi to stay so she could see the miracle change her mother was going to manifest in her life. Andi was simply encouraged she was going to seek some help.

Her bigger dilemma, however, was that stubborn man next door whom she was certain loved her as much as she loved him. If he were any other man, she wouldn't be so certain. But he wasn't any other man. He was uniquely Colton. A little bit of a strange bird and so was she.

He hadn't denied he loved her. Neither had he denied she was the woman who'd always been unavailable. Of those things she was certain. What she didn't know was how to get through to him before he headed back out tomorrow for danger and uncertainty. As her grandfather Mitchell had been fond of saying, you could lead a horse to water but you couldn't make him drink. Apparently the same held true for a stubborn jackass.

COLTON WAS STRETCHED OUT on the guest bed trying to get his head into his book, to no avail, when his cell phone rang. He checked the display. He'd been expecting this call. It had taken longer than he'd expected.

He answered. "What took you so long?"

Rion's voice had just a bit of static on the other end. "Thought I'd give you enough time to hang yourself."

"Very funny."

"Well, as the official man of the house, inabsentia, I'm demanding to know when you're going to make an honest woman of my sister."

"You're kidding, right?"

"Not really. The honest woman part, yeah, but man, how long is it going to take you to own up to how you feel about her and do something about it? I even made damn sure my leave was denied and yours was granted—"

WTF? "How'd you do that?"

He could almost see Rion shrug over the phone. "I've got connections." Colton didn't doubt it. That was pretty much the way Rion operated. "So, I made sure you were there thinking there was no way in hell you'd let her go through with marrying that guy Blanton when you've only been in love with her yourself for the last several years."

Colton had always been so careful to guard his feelings about Andi, but apparently not careful enough. They were past the point of denial. "How did you know?"

"Good God, it wasn't hard to tell. And she's been in love with you for forever. I have never seen two more pathetic people dance around one another. Andi brings a little spontaneity to you, obviously if you took off with her like that, and you offer my little sister some stability."

"What pop psychology book did you get that from?"

"I got that from your sister. Mattie's a pretty smart chick. You ought to try talking to her now and then."

"Speaking of my sister. I understand you kissed her."

"You're a day late and a dollar short, Colton. That was way back when and I'm betting you did a whole helluva lot more than kiss my sister this past week so you might not want to go there. So, what's this I hear that she wants to get married and you don't?"

"Did she call you?"

"Nah. Mattie did. But don't try and sidetrack here. What's your problem? You love her and she loves you."

"You know what it's like where we are. What it's like for the families left behind."

"Colton, for such a smart guy sometimes you can be a total dumb-ass. It is exactly because of what it's like where we are that you should seize whatever chance you have to be happy and to make someone else happy while you can because you damn well may never have the opportunity again. You know, you're damn well treating my sister the way my mother does. You're trying in your heavy-handed way to protect her without considering what it is she wants, what will make her happy. She's loved you for more than half her life so how do you think walking away from her is the best thing for her?"

Colton was all for researching the hell out of things but he also tended to get tunnel vision. He'd never examined it from the perspective Rion had just put forth. It felt like a sucker punch to the gut. Rion was right. Colton was no better than Daisy in trying to direct Andi's life and not trusting that she was capable of making her own decisions.

"You want us to wait until you can be at the wedding?"

"Hell, no. Have someone videotape it and I'll watch it on the computer. I think I'm allergic to weddings. That was yet another reason my leave was denied."

"Later."

"Hey, Colton—"

"Yeah?"

"Welcome to the family. And just think, bro, my mother is going to be your mother-in-law."

Rion's laughter was still ringing on the other end when he hung up on Colton.

For the first time Colton really allowed himself to imagine a life with Andi, unfettered by his own denial. He double-timed it down the hall. The meat loaf smelled great. Everything in life was suddenly great. His mother was putzing around the kitchen when he came in and caught her up in a hug. "Listen, y'all are going to have to enjoy dinner without the pleasure of my and Andi's company tonight."

"If I'm giving up my son's last evening home he better at least be doing what he needs to do."

"How would you feel about packing up my and Andi's portion of dinner in a picnic basket?"

"Is that ruby ring part of the picnic?" she hard-lined him.

"Yes, ma'am, it is." He started out of the kitchen, then paused. "Oh, and Mom, do us all a favor and keep Daisy occupied."

ANDI SLIPPED INTO A pretty spring dress that came off equally easy. She was also wearing that front-hook bra Colton was so fond of. She read his text for about the twentieth time since she'd received it an hour ago.

You're invited for a Grand Adventure. 7:15 @ tree house. Bring candles.

The summer they were twelve, Colton and Rion had built a clubhouse in a sprawling oak on the back line of the Sawyer property. Their dads had helped them and the boys had spent hours during the summer hanging out there. Long after they'd outgrown the clubhouse, Mr. Sawyer had kept it up, replacing boards as they rotted. A couple of years ago, when he was home on leave, Rion had overhauled the clubhouse himself. He'd said it was because he was bored with nothing else to do but she suspected it was more of an homage to the memory of a man who'd been surrogate father to them after their own father had died.

As a kid, Andi had begged to be allowed in their sanctuary and had always been denied entry. As a defiant teenager, she'd been up there several times when Colton and Rion were away at school. And she'd loved it because it made her feel close to Colton. Now she was embarking on yet another Grand Adventure and this time it was the sacred clubhouse. She had a good feeling.

After brushing on some lip gloss, she headed down the hall. She'd already told her mother she wouldn't be joining the rest of them for dinner. Her mother would've probably had plenty to say, if she'd been speaking to her. Sometimes you had to be thankful for small blessings. And this was another one because her mother was still sequestered in her room and wouldn't see where Andi went.

She slipped out the side door and walked down the block, cutting up on the other side of the Sawyer house into the backyard. Dusk had quickly settled into dark but she picked her way by the light of the quarter moon to the sprawling oak. She smelled him, sensed him, felt him, before she saw him leaning beneath the canopy of branches.

"You came," he said, putting his arms around her and hauling her close for a hug.

"Of course I did. You know I can't resist a Grand

Adventure." She lightly kissed him, unsure of exactly where they stood.

"Oh, is that the only reason you came?" he said, but he kept his arms around her, still holding her close.

"Well, I was still on the fence but about halfway across the yard I was pretty sure I smelled meat loaf, mashed potatoes and your mother's gingered carrots, so here I am. When are we going to eat?"

He chuckled quietly and released her, sweeping his arm toward the ladder leading up. "Ladies first. Be careful going up."

"Are you kidding? I used to climb this thing in the dark all the time. In fact this is my favorite time to be out here because it's getting warm but the mosquitoes aren't feasting in full force."

"Did you bring the candles?"

"Of course I did. And matches too in case you forgot them."

When she got to the top, she was surprised to see he'd spread several blankets on the floor and there were a couple of throw pillows. Rion and Colton had been lanky adolescents when they built the clubhouse and now she and Colton were adults, not to mention he was a fairly big man. With the picnic basket and pillows, it made for tight quarters but tight quarters suited her just fine since it meant she was that much closer to him.

She passed the candles to him and he placed them in the far corners before he lit them. Moonlight filtered through the tree's still-bare branches. It was one of the most romantic setups she thought she'd ever seen.

"I'd suggest we eat first, so you're not about to expire from hunger."

"You're just too funny," she said.

"A lot of people don't see that in me." He was quiet and serious.

"That's because they don't love you like I do." She would beat him over the head with it.

"I suspect that's true enough" was his only rejoinder.

He passed her a plate and took one himself. Backs propped against the pillows and the clubhouse wall, they ate. For a measure of time it was merely the occasional clink of a fork against a plate. Andi finally broke the silence. "Your mother makes the best meat loaf. I wonder if she'd give me the recipe?"

"I'm sure she would."

"This is your favorite meal, isn't it?"

"Yep. It's hard to beat. How'd it go with your mother?"

"Pretty much the way we both thought it would. She's currently not speaking to me."

"Maybe that's not a bad thing."

"Great minds think alike. It was the same thought I had."

They finished eating and Colton stacked the plates back in the basket. "Come here," he said.

She willingly settled on his lap. He wrapped his

arms around her and she snuggled into his chest. "Mmm, this is nice," she said, a good feeling flowing through her that had nothing to do with the meal she'd just consumed and everything to do with the man who held her in his arms as if he'd never let her go.

"So you like the Grand Adventure I planned?"

She nuzzled her lips against his neck. "So far, so good."

He shifted slightly, "Uh, honey, can you not do that right now because it makes it hard for me to think."

She shifted deliberately against his burgeoning arousal beneath her. "It makes lots of things hard."

"Andi," he said warningly.

"Okay, I'll behave."

"Just for now. Just for a little bit." He cleared his throat and caught her left hand in his hand. "Ah, I see you took off Blanton's rock."

"Yeah, once I got home and could safely store it. I just didn't want to lose it."

"You know, I've been told that for a smart guy I can be a real dumb-ass."

She laughed softly. He had to have talked with her brother. "When did you talk to Rion?"

"How do you know I talked to him?"

"Because that sounds exactly like him."

Colton laughed quietly. "Yeah, it was Rion. We talked this afternoon." He rested his head against her hair and said quietly, "I love you, Andi. I have for a long time. You were the woman who was never available. By the time you were old enough that our ages didn't matter, I was being sent to a war zone and then you were dating Blanton. And I always thought what your mother wanted for you was what you wanted, to stay here in Savannah."

She wasn't exactly sure what had turned his tide for him, she was just damn glad to hear it. "So does this mean you're going to marry me?"

"Dammit, woman, would you give a man a chance to say his piece?"

"Okay. I'm sorry. Speak, Major."

He reached to his left and grabbed something. "Well, since there's an empty spot on your finger, why don't you try this on for size?"

In the flickering candlelight and the moonlight sifting down through the branches she opened the box to see the Sawyer promise ruby. Of course she'd heard about it. He took the box from her and pulled out the ring. "Will you marry me?"

A quiet joy, a newfound contentment welled inside her. "Of course." He slid the ring onto her finger. It was a bit of a snug fit, but that was good since she wouldn't have to worry about losing it. "How soon?"

"Can you plan a wedding in three months?"

"Three months? Are you crazy?"

"Okay, we'll make it longer if you need longer."

It had taken years for them to get to this point.

She wasn't going to trust him not to come up with some logical, rational ridiculous reason to change his mind. "No. There's no way I'm waiting three months to marry you. Tomorrow."

"But that means we'd just have to rush down to the courthouse because my flight leaves around two tomorrow. Don't you want to wait and make sure?"

"I've been waiting over half my life for this. I don't want you to change your mind."

"Hey, I'm not the one with the history of being a runaway bride."

She nudged him in his side with her elbow. "You would have to bring that up."

"It just happens to be fresh on my memory…since it was just a few days ago. Seriously, honey, you know if we get married tomorrow everyone will speculate we've been having an affair while you were engaged to Blanton."

"Colton, I don't want to besmirch your reputation but if I cared what people thought, I'd have never climbed out that window in the first place. The only thing I care about is you. We can wait three months or we can wait a year and the same tongues are going to wag with the same speculation."

"Then let's get married tomorrow. You know we won't have time for a honeymoon."

He wasn't the only one who could be practical. With the moonlight sifting through the branches in a random pattern, she tugged her dress over her head.

The cool air of early spring raised gooseflesh on her, but Colton would take care of that soon enough.

"Well, I say we get a jump start on that right now."

Epilogue

Three and a half months later...

"I THINK THAT'S EVERYTHING," Andi said as Colton attached her car to the tow bar.

"You know, anytime—" her mother began for the tenth time that morning.

"I know I can come home anytime." She looked across to her mother-in-law and sister-in-law. "And in a month, the three of you are going to be coming up for a visit." She reached over and hugged her mother. "I'm so proud of you, Mom."

Her mother had been in therapy for nearly three months now with tremendous results. She was still overprotective and neurotic but it was far, far better than it had been. And she was even cordial to her new son-in-law.

"I guess we'd better get on the road," Colton said quietly. She could tell he was loath to interrupt but they had to make Natick in two days and he had to get back to work.

There were hugs and more than a few tears as she and her husband climbed into the cab of the moving van. They could've hired movers but they'd both thought it would be fun to drive up the East Coast together.

Andi was crying as they pulled out of the driveway and she looked in the big mirror outside her door and saw her mother, Martha Anne and Mattie all crying, as well. She rolled down the window and called out, "I'll email, I'll call, I'll text, just not every day. I love you." She pulled her head back inside.

"Are you okay, honey?"

"I'm fine. I'm happy, it's just a little…"

"I know."

And that was the great thing about Colton, her husband, he did know.

"Here we are starting on another Grand Adventure," she said, swiping at her eyes. And she was okay. Her tears were a combination of sadness around a fond farewell and excitement over a new beginning. But she was exactly where she wanted to be with exactly the man meant for her. She reached over and touched his arm. "I love you, Colton Sawyer."

"I know," he said. "And I love you, Andi Sawyer. You nailed it early on. We're going to have a lifetime of Grand Adventures together."

* * * * *

COMING NEXT MONTH

Available March 29, 2011

#603 SECOND TIME LUCKY
Spring Break
Debbi Rawlins

#604 HIGHLY CHARGED!
Uniformly Hot!
Joanne Rock

#605 WHAT MIGHT HAVE BEEN
Kira Sinclair

#606 LONG SLOW BURN
Checking E-Males
Isabel Sharpe

#607 SHE WHO DARES, WINS
Candace Havens

#608 CAUGHT ON CAMERA
Meg Maguire

You can find more information on upcoming
Harlequin® titles, free excerpts and more at
www.HarlequinInsideRomance.com.

HBCNM0311

REQUEST YOUR FREE BOOKS!
2 FREE NOVELS PLUS 2 FREE GIFTS!

red-hot reads!

YES! Please send me 2 FREE Harlequin® Blaze® novels and my 2 FREE gifts (gifts are worth about $10). After receiving them, if I don't wish to receive any more books, I can return the shipping statement marked "cancel." If I don't cancel, I will receive 6 brand-new novels every month and be billed just $4.24 per book in the U.S. or $4.71 per book in Canada. That's a saving of at least 15% off the cover price. It's quite a bargain. Shipping and handling is just 50¢ per book in the U.S. and 75¢ per book in Canada.* I understand that accepting the 2 free books and gifts places me under no obligation to buy anything. I can always return a shipment and cancel at any time. Even if I never buy another book, the two free books and gifts are mine to keep forever.

151/351 HDN FC4T

Name	(PLEASE PRINT)	
Address		Apt. #
City	State/Prov.	Zip/Postal Code

Signature (if under 18, a parent or guardian must sign)

Mail to the **Reader Service:**
IN U.S.A.: P.O. Box 1867, Buffalo, NY 14240-1867
IN CANADA: P.O. Box 609, Fort Erie, Ontario L2A 5X3

Not valid for current subscribers to Harlequin Blaze books.

Want to try two free books from another line?
Call 1-800-873-8635 or visit www.ReaderService.com.

* Terms and prices subject to change without notice. Prices do not include applicable taxes. Sales tax applicable in N.Y. Canadian residents will be charged applicable taxes. Offer not valid in Quebec. This offer is limited to one order per household. All orders subject to credit approval. Credit or debit balances in a customer's account(s) may be offset by any other outstanding balance owed by or to the customer. Please allow 4 to 6 weeks for delivery. Offer available while quantities last.

Your Privacy—The Reader Service is committed to protecting your privacy. Our Privacy Policy is available online at www.ReaderService.com or upon request from the Reader Service.

We make a portion of our mailing list available to reputable third parties that offer products we believe may interest you. If you prefer that we not exchange your name with third parties, or if you wish to clarify or modify your communication preferences, please visit us at www.ReaderService.com/consumerchoice or write to us at Reader Service Preference Service, P.O. Box 9062, Buffalo, NY 14269. Include your complete name and address.

HB11

*Selene wanted nothing to do with the father of her son,
Alex; but Aristedes had other plans...that included them.*

*Read on for an sneak peek from
THE SARANTOS SECRET BABY by Olivia Gates,
available April 2011, only from Harlequin Desire.*

"You were right to turn my marriage offer down," Aristedes said.

And Selene found her voice at last, found the words that
would not betray the blow he'd dealt her. "Thanks for let-
ting me know. You didn't have to come all the way here,
though. You could have just let it go. I left yesterday with
the understanding that this case is closed."

Before the hot needles behind her eyes could dissolve
into an unforgivable display of stupidity and weakness, she
began to close the door.

The door stopped against an immovable object. His flat palm.

"I can't accept that." His voice was low, leashed.

What did her tormentor mean now? Was he ending one
game only to start another?

She raised eyes as bruised as her self-respect to his,
found nothing there but solemnity and determination.

Before she could voice her confusion, he elaborated. "I
never let anything go unless I'm certain it's unworkable. I
realize I made you an unworkable offer, and that's why I'm
withdrawing it. I'm here to offer something else. A work-
ability study."

She leaned against the door, thankful for its support and
partial shield. "Your son and I are not a business venture
you can test for feasibility."

His gaze grew deeper, made her feel as if he was trying
to delve into her mind, take control of it. "It's actually the

other way around. I'm the one who would be tested."

She shook her head. "Why bother? I know—and *you* know—you're not workable. Not with me."

His spectacular eyebrows lowered over eyes she felt were emitting silver hypnosis. "You're right again. Neither you nor I have any reason to believe that isn't the truth. The only truth. It might be best for both you and Alex to never hear from me again, to forget I exist. But then again, maybe not. I'm only asking for the chance for both of us to find out for certain. You believe I'm unworkable in any personal relationship. I've lived my life based on that belief about myself. I never really had reason to question it. But I have one now. In fact, I have two."

Find out what happens in
THE SARANTOS SECRET BABY by Olivia Gates,
available April 2011, only from Harlequin Desire.

Harlequin® *Blaze*™

red-hot reads

Sunny, sensual Hawaiian spring break…again!

Three best girlfriends are recapturing an amazing spring-break
vacation they had a decade ago.

First on the beach is former attorney and all-around good girl
Mia Butterfield. Meeting up with her boyfriend of old is a bust,
so she's shocked when her hero turns out to be someone she'd
never have expected…

Find out who it is in
SECOND TIME LUCKY
by acclaimed author
Debbi Rawlins

Available from Harlequin Blaze® April 2011

Part of the sensual miniseries,
Spring Break

Part 2: Delicious Do-Over (May)

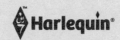

Harlequin®

A *Romance* FOR EVERY MOOD™

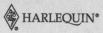

INTRIGUE

THE NEW EQUALIZERS

Melissa Shepherd's life shatters when her three-year-old niece is abducted. There's only one man, Equalizer Jonathan Foley, who might be able to help. He has refused to commit to her emotionally, but there's no way he can refuse to help the only woman who has ever come close to touching his heart.

Will Jonathan be able to find the child and protect Melissa, while fighting his own feelings?

FIND OUT IN...

MISSING

BY

DEBRA WEBB

Available April 12, 2011, wherever you buy books.